Bear the Heat

(Fire Bears, Book 3)

T. S. JOYCE

Bear the Heat

ISBN-13: 978-1540775078
ISBN-10: 1540775070
Copyright © 2015, T. S. Joyce
First electronic publication: June 2015

T. S. Joyce
www. tsjoyce.com

NOTE FROM THE AUTHOR:

This book is a work of fiction. The names, characters, places, and incidents are products of the writer's imagination or have been used fictitiously and are not to be construed as real. Any resemblance to persons, living or dead, actual events, locale or organizations is entirely coincidental. The author does not have any control over and does not assume any responsibility for third-party websites or their content.

Published in the United States of America

First digital publication: June 2015
First print publication: December 2016

Editing: Corinne DeMaagd

ONE

A thunderous booming sounded against the walls of Boone Keller's cabin. Muscles jerking, he sat up in bed. The pounding rattled his front door a second time, and he lurched for the bedroom light switch. The illumination burned his eyes, and he winced and shielded his face from the harsh lights above.

The knocking was louder now, and if the person on the other side of that door didn't quit, they were going to splinter the wooden barrier that stood between him and the woods outside.

"I'm coming," he called out, stumbling for the living room. A curse tumbled from his lips for the arm of the couch he slammed into, then he threw open the door.

Cody stood there, wide-eyed, and if Boone wasn't mistaken, terrified. He'd never seen his older brother scared before.

"Take my boy and keep him safe," Cody said in a desperate voice as he shoved his five-year-old son, Aaron, into Boone's arms.

The rattling of automatic gunfire echoed through the woods.

"What's happening?" Boone asked, scanning the woods as he clutched a whimpering Aaron tight to his chest.

"They've found us."

"Who?"

Cody backed off the front porch, and his piercing blue eyes dimmed with sadness. "Everyone."

Rory, Cody's mate, lay crumpled in the yard, her eyes fixed on him. "Boone, save him," she said in a hoarse whisper.

Adrenaline dumped into his veins as he raked his horrified gaze over her open stomach. Crimson stained her white sundress.

"Cody?" he uttered as he ripped his attention away from Rory's suffering and searched his front yard. Cody had disappeared into the shadows as if he'd never *existed at all.*

"Run," his alpha's voice whispered on the wind.

Panting with panic, heart pounding against his sternum, Boone held Aaron tight against his chest and ran for the safety of the woods. This territory was his. He knew every nook and cranny, every rock crevice and cliff.

Branches whipped his face and shoulders as he ducked and dodged around them to protect Aaron. To the left, running parallel, Gage was herding his mate, Leah, and their two cubs in the same direction. Blue moonlight covered them in eerie shadows, but he knew their scent. They were his crew, and they were here, running with him toward safety.

"Where's Dade?" Boone yelled, his voice sounding hollow against the onslaught of peppering gunfire.

Gage didn't answer, didn't even turn his head.

Aaron was crying now, frail shoulders shaking. He hadn't hit his first growth spurt yet and was tiny still, in need of protection.

"It's okay," Boone panted out as his limbs became heavy. "You're safe with me, little bear." He hoped his words sounded more confident than he felt.

He slowed, struggling against the waterlogged

sensation his legs had adopted. His feet dragged through the pine needles that blanketed the forest floor, and when he turned to Gage to ask for help, a spray of bullets echoed through the wilderness and bowed Gage and his family forward with pained cries.

"Gage!" Boone yelled, desperation clawing at his throat.

Turning away in horror, he laid eyes on Ma, kneeling in the dirt, humming an off-key tune as she rocked back and forth, back and forth. She was hunched over something, so he dragged his heavy body closer and searched the ground in front of her. Dade and Bruiser lay beside each other, heads resting in Ma's lap, eyes clouded, staring vacantly into the space between them, faces smattered with blood. Quinn lay alone in front of them, white dress tattered and knees bloodied. She was struggling on her last breath, her lungs rattling with fluid.

"Oh, God!" Boone cried, shaking his head. "Ma, run!"

"Too late for me, my Boone. My heart died with my boys." A crack of gunfire sounded and Ma jolted straight up, a look of shock and pain in her blue eyes. A red stain spread across her chest as she whispered,

"Save her."

Her? Boone looked down in his arms, but he wasn't holding Aaron anymore. He was holding Cora.

"I'm scared," Cora whispered, blond hair whipping about in the wind, hazel eyes as round as the full moon.

"You should be," Shayna whispered from the shadows. "Boone brought you to the Reaper." She stepped out from behind a towering spruce tree, handgun trained on the woman in his arms.

"It's okay," Cora whispered just before Shayna pulled the trigger.

The sound of metal cracking against the firing pin was deafening, and Cora slid from his arms.

"Nooo!" he screamed, the word transforming into a roar.

Boone woke up yelling, throat hoarse, body rigid from fighting in his mind. His bedroom was dark, but the blue moonlight filtered through the open window as the chilly fall breeze brushed across his damp skin.

Supernatural electricity zinged up his arms and legs, sparking against his muscles until he seized. Back arching against the tossed bed sheets, he began his Change just as the first whisper reached his ear.

"Laura will be so pissed she missed this," someone murmured, laughter in their voice.

Helplessly, Boone dragged his gaze to the window, where a cellphone camera showed a terrifying reflection of himself—veins bulging, skin ripping, fur sprouting, screaming...roaring.

Fury blasted through him in the final moments of his Change. He was a territorial hellion. These intruders had come onto his land, witnessed another one of his nightmares...the ones where he couldn't save the people he cared about. They saw him vulnerable. Recorded it to be replayed over and over again.

No. *No, no, no.*

Boone stood up on his hind legs and roared. Scared whimpers from the spies, and that was better. They should know.

Boone Keller was a monster—a death bringer—and they should see their end coming.

He dropped to all fours, claws raking against the carpet and lips curling back over his long canines.

And then he charged.

TWO

Cora Wright nudged an oversize pair of sunglasses higher up her nose with her shoulder and dodged a pair of rowdy kids running from their harried mother on the sidewalk of Main Street. She gripped the two plastic cups of fragrant coffee tighter and smiled her understanding as the mother apologized and rushed past. Cora liked kids and volunteered for an afterschool reading program once a week at a local elementary school, so she understood perfectly well how rambunctious they could be.

The sidewalk was crowded for this early in the morning, but she shouldn't be surprised. Tourists rose early in Breckenridge, as did the locals to open their souvenir shops and restaurants.

She bustled under the hand-painted *Grand Opening* sign and through the front door of Mack's Gourmet Candy Shop. The smell of fresh melted chocolate, fruit fillings, and assorted nuts was enough to lift her spirits. The sight of her raven-haired, tattoo-covered cousin, Joslyn "Jos" Mack, who talked animatedly to a customer near a working taffy-stretching machine, drew a sigh of relief from her lips. Talking to Jos would make her feel better. She had a way with wise words and advice, and a soft way of thinking that Cora needed about now.

"Whoa," Jos said as she approached the counter. "You look like shit."

Or maybe not.

"Thanks a lot." Cora smiled politely at the man at the counter who took his crinkling package of chocolate Danishes and sidled around her. "I brought you coffee in exchange for a shoulder to lean on."

"Woman, look at that sign over there."

Cora squinted through the dark tint of her sunglasses and read the chalkboard with the neon lettering. *Best coffee in town.*

"Well, how was I supposed to know you served

coffee? Or breakfast for that matter? This is a candy shop, and this is my first time in here."

"Is it from the cake shop?" Jos asked, eyeing the steaming cups.

"Maybe." Cora handed her one and took a sip of her own.

The shop was bustling three strong, but no one seemed ready to check out, so Cora double-timed it around the counter and took the seat Jos pointed to. "Lay it on me. Except if this is about assface. I can't handle him this morning."

"Why? What's wrong?"

"Nothing. Just nervous about passing the fire inspection. Since this building was remodeled, they have to come in and make sure it's safe and I'm not violating any fire safety codes. It's the last obstacle until we are officially *officially* open for business. Wait, this is about assface, isn't it?"

"You know, I'm not even going to tell you to stop calling him that anymore." Cora swallowed hard. "Jos, we're really done this time."

Jos's dark eyebrows lifted high, and she leaned forward and lowered her voice. "What did he do?"

Cora shook her head, unable to put words to the

heinous betrayal Eddie had laid on her heart.

"He cheated again, didn't he?"

Pain slashed through Cora's middle at the memory of the night she'd caught him with another woman. "Yeah. I told him to get out that night, but he said it was his house, and if I wanted to split up, I had to leave."

"What? You pay half that rent. He cheated. He should move out."

"Yeah, he didn't even make the girl leave. She was some tourist, I think. I've never seen her before. She was in the kitchen, drinking coffee out of my favorite mug while I packed."

Jos's dark eyes flashed with fury, and she ran her hand roughly through her short, spiked hair. "I don't get you Cora. You are strong as all get-out when it comes to everything but Eddie. Why have you let it get this far?"

"That's not what I need to hear right now."

"Okay, when did this happen?"

"Last week. I've been staying at the condo up the hill, trying to get my head on straight."

"What? Why didn't you tell me? You could've been staying in our extra bedroom."

"I don't want to inconvenience you and Meredith. You are basically on your honeymoon, and I'd be intruding with my boxes of Kleenexes and patheticness."

"Patheticness isn't a word."

Cora sighed and leveled her a look over the rim of her sunglasses. "Not helping."

Jos slid the glasses from Cora's face and cupped her cheek. "Darlin', you can't be hiding behind those lenses forever. That man doesn't deserve your tears, and you work in television. Puffy eyes don't become a badass like you. You should've left him the first time he pulled this."

Another wave of self-loathing slid over Cora's shoulders as she warmed her fingers around the coffee cup. "I really should've. Eddie was a waste of three years."

Jos turned and rang up a customer, then leaned against the counter and dug her phone from her back pocket. "You know what'll make you feel better?"

"What?" Cora asked, frowning at her cousin as she poked around on the screen of her cell.

"Taking your mind off Eddie. You aren't the only one having a bad week. Have you seen this? It started going viral this morning."

"What is it?" she said, squinting at the dark video.

"You know the Kellers?"

"Of course, I do."

"Someone snuck onto Boone Keller's property and videotaped him in the throes of a nightmare."

Horrified, Cora watched Boone kick off the covers to his bed. The camera was held by a shaky hand, and it was dark, but with the moonlight, she could easily make him out. "I shouldn't be watching this," she murmured, but she couldn't take her eyes from the man as he arched his back against his mattress and let off a long, low, feral snarl. What a horrible violation of this man—this shifter's—privacy.

She gasped as he screamed the word *no* and lurched awake, only to go rigid as a giant, blond grizzly ripped from his body with a smattering of pops that sounded like snapping bones. His eyes reflected strangely in the moonlight as he stood on his hind legs and leveled the camera with a wild glare, then charged toward the open window. There was muttering on the tape, too low for her to make out on the cell, even at high volume, but the shaking camera documented a terrified run through thick woods. The tape cut off half a minute later.

Cora barely registered the draft from the open door as she and Jos stared at the glowing screen.

"Over a million hits already and look at all those comments," Jos said low. "It doesn't look like he meant to shift into a bear, and that lack of control has people freaking out."

A man cleared his throat on the other side of the counter, and Cora froze. Cody and Gage Keller stared at her and Jos with matching, unamused expressions, while Boone Keller himself stood off to the side, looking down at the legs of one of the iron tables in Jos's candy shop. His mouth was set in a grim line. Double shit.

"I v-voted for you to be reinstated as firemen," Jos said, stumbling over her words. "I'm pro-shifter."

"Much appreciated," Cody, alpha of the Breck Crew, said in a deep voice. "You mind if we get started?"

Jos inhaled harshly and pursed her lips. "Go ahead."

Gage and Cody strode off toward the back room,

but as Boone passed, he paused beside her. His blond, normally shoulder-length hair had been pulled back in a band, and his piercing blue gaze lifted slowly to hers. Clad in a casual navy blue fireman's uniform and thick boots, he looked tall and dashing despite the hard set of his lips.

"You smell sad, Cora. Are those tears for me?"

Petrified into place, she shook her head and breathed out, "No. They were for Eddie."

His eyes tightened slightly before he turned away from her and strode after his brothers.

"Son of a hairy gobshite," Jos whispered. "They totally busted us watching that awful video. I'm so screwed."

Cora wiped her cheeks, but she didn't have any tears. Just puffy eyes and damp lashes. Bear shifters could smell sadness? "Maybe it'll be fine. The Kellers are professionals. Maybe they'll still pass you."

"Yeah right," Jos muttered. "People don't do that kind of stuff anymore. They're going to fail me. I know it."

Jos had worked so hard for this shop. She and her wife, Meredith, had been saving for years to open a business right on Main Street, and now that dream was facing this obstacle? It was her fault. "I'll fix this."

Shoving her sunglasses in the purse slung across her shoulder, Cora made her way to the back room, her hiking boots squeaking against the clean, white tile floors.

The brothers were talking low in the back room, but it sounded like a conversation about how close some of the boxes were to the fire exit, and definitely not about her and Jos's asshattery watching that stupid video.

"'Scuse me, Boone?"

The somber man slid a glance to her. "What?" His voice chilled her blood and sent gooseflesh skittering across her arms.

She scrunched up her nose and asked, "Can I talk to you for a minute?"

"This isn't a social call, Cora. I'm working." The way he said her name slid warmth over her skin. It sounded so familiar coming from his lips, as if they'd known each other for years instead of officially meeting a couple of minutes ago.

"Please," she said.

His gaze dipped to her lips, and he frowned. "Yeah, okay." He brushed Cody's arm with his knuckles. "I'll be right back."

Cody grunted a caveman-like sound, as if he gave zero figs if his brother left to talk to her or not. Geez, it was intimidating being in a small room with these three men. And not just because they were harboring giant brown bears inside of them either. They each commanded attention and made the room feel much smaller than it actually was—and all without any apparent effort. Especially Boone, who somehow loomed more like a giant with every step he took toward her.

She led him into a narrow hallway that led to Jos and Meredith's office and turned around, where she ran smack into his chest.

"Jesus," he muttered, grabbing her arms and steadying her. Then he yanked his hands away like she was a hot branding iron. "What do you want?" he asked, the word sharp as a blade.

Boone crossed his arms over his chest like a protective shield, and Cora tried and failed not to gawk at his flexed pecs and biceps under the thin material of his shirt. Down one arm was a sleeve of tattoos, lacking any color save black ink, in intricate designs she couldn't understand. She was staring.

Cora cleared her throat and forced her eyes to meet his. "I'm sorry. You know, for earlier. I shouldn't have looked at that stupid video. It was awful that happened to you. I'm...sorry."

"You already said that."

"Well, I double mean it."

"Who's Eddie?"

Cora opened her mouth and clacked it closed again, frowning so hard her forehead hurt. That wasn't what she'd expected him to ask.

His golden blond eyebrows wrenched high as he waited.

"He's nobody to me anymore."

"But he hurt you." A statement, not a question.

"Anyway, I just didn't want you to fail Jos's shop because of that really bad lapse in judgement."

"So, you pulled me away from the inspection to let me know you're sorry you were caught—not to actually talk to me?"

"Yeah. No." She pursed her lips and narrowed her eyes at him, feeling unbalanced. "I don't know."

"Don't worry about it." Boone twitched his head like he'd been wounded. "I wouldn't have failed a shop for personal reasons, you know. That's not me, and it's not my brothers either. Thought you would've known that."

"Wait," she said, grabbing his arm as he turned to leave.

He yanked it back, just as he'd done before. "What, Cora?" His eyes sparked with fury.

"How would I have known that? I don't even know you."

Boone nodded slowly, and a humorless smile took his lips as he hooked his hands on his waist and looked at the ground. "That's right. You don't. But you defend me and *my kind* enough. I thought you, of all people, would see me—us—as good, decent people. Not just mindless animals."

He turned and left her in the hallway. She made an exasperated sound deep in her throat, utterly baffled at the exchange. She did defend them, often and publicly. She worked for the news and put her career on the line to point out when the anti-shifter rioters were being dick-pastries. How rude that he questioned her support. She'd been the loudest one at all the rallies when they first came out a few months ago, risking her job to loudly support their side. The right side. The side of justice and fairness. The side of equal rights and the right to live safely like the rest of the public.

"Jerk," she muttered.

"I heard that," Boone called.

"Shit," she murmured.

"Heard that, too."

An angry little screech marched up the back of her throat, and she left in a huff. Stupid bear hearing. Jos was with a customer, so Cora waved a frustrated goodbye and yanked her coffee off the counter, then made her way out the door. She'd call her cousin later, but right now, her temper was as hot as a roman candle. She could blame that on her Irish heritage, but really, it was Boone's fault. As if she needed to be called out by a stranger. Her insides were breaking apart after Eddie had stomped on her devotion. Work had given her a few career-smudging "mental health" days off, and her cameraman, Carl, had jumped right on over to Ivanna Prichard, who was an intern after Cora's job and openly anti-shifter. And now Boone Keller was giving her shit? Confusing and sexy, the stone-bodied Viking had given her grief like they'd been childhood friends.

That exchange with Boone bothered her the

most, but she had no guess why. He was just a man. A stranger with big muscles and a tattoo she wanted to decipher, but still.

He was nobody to her, just like Eddie.

THREE

Boone tossed a regretful look at the door Cora had disappeared through. "Dammit," he muttered with a sigh. That wasn't how he'd planned for their first conversation to go. No, scratch that. He hadn't planned on there being a first conversation. Cora couldn't know about him anymore than she already did.

But he felt like a total dick talking to her like that.

"What did you do to piss Cora Wright off?" Cody asked in that disapproving tone he adopted when he or his brothers did something stupid in public.

"Don't act like you didn't hear."

Gage shoved Boone's shoulder. "Dude, we need her to stay on our side. What's your problem? I could see plain as day she's hurting over something. Don't you know anything about women? You don't pick at them when they're hurt. Doesn't matter if they're humans or she-bears."

"I should apologize," Boone said. Geez, he sucked. He *should* let her be pissed and hate him, but already, he was planning ways to see her again and make sure she didn't think he was a "jerk." His brothers called him names every thirty seconds, but they never carried the sting the insult from her lips had. With a frustrated growl, he told Cody, "I'll meet you out front."

Quick as a whip, he purchased a small bag of hand-dipped chocolate-covered cherries from the shop owner, then jogged out of the candy store. Cora's scent was easy enough to follow, thanks to the boner-inducing strawberry and mint shampoo she'd washed her hair with. Most perfumes hurt his sensitive nose and gave him headaches, but her fruity smell made him want to shove his nose in her hair and only breath the oxygen saturated with her scent.

Boone drew up short as he turned the corner and saw Cora sitting on a bench in an alleyway off the main sidewalk. It was chilly out, and even with her heavy coat covering the top half of her, she was shivering. Tight jeans clung to her legs like a second skin, and her hiking boots were so damned cute all tied up over her pants. When he watched her on the news, her shoulder length hair was always curled and perfectly in place, but today, she'd worn it straight and pulled back into a ponytail. The shortest of her hairs stuck out of her hairband in little spikes he wanted to nibble.

Nibble? Boone didn't do nibbling. He bit. Hard. He should leave.

"What do you want?" she asked him, making it too late to run.

Boone's heart banged against his chest as he approached and sat down beside her. "Here." He handed her the bag of sweets.

"What are these for?"

"An apology."

Cora sniffled and laughed thickly. "It seems all we've done since we met is apologize to each other."

He twitched his head and stared at a row of dried summer plants in colorful pots against the brick building they were facing. "You want to talk about it?"

Cora laughed again and shook her head. "No. You

already think I'm silly enough."

"I don't. And I'm a good listener and really fuckin' good with secrets. Plus, we don't know each other and may never see each other again. I'm the best person to unload on."

"Aren't you working?"

"We're passing your friend's shop, you know. All she has to do is move some of the boxes from in front of the fire exit and watch her maximum occupancy. We mostly do this with new buildings and businesses so we can familiarize ourselves with the layout, in case we ever need to fight a fire there."

"You're passing her?"

"Yeah, her shop wasn't ever in jeopardy from us."

Cora pulled open the crackling paper bag and handed him a chocolate cherry. "Jos is my cousin. We grew up together, and I was scared I'd ruined it for her. She's worked for a really long time to open up the candy shop."

Boone popped the treat into his mouth and nodded his approval as the dark chocolate converged with the tart fruit on his tongue. "Who's Eddie?"

"Eddie would be Edward Bills, a writer for the town newspaper. He's also my recently demoted ex."

Green fog drifted through him. He inhaled deeply to settle his snarling bear and said, "Mmm. Why was he demoted? If you're crying, it means you still care for him."

"I care for what we could've been." She brushed a finger under her sunglasses and leaned back against the bench. "We were together three years, and I thought for sure he was going to propose any day. Problem was, I couldn't see it at the time, but I cared about him a lot more than he cared for me."

"Did he leave you?"

"No. He moved on, but he didn't have the decency to leave first."

Boone leaned forward and rested his elbows on his knees to calm his shaking knee. He wanted to crack the fucker's skull. "He cheated?"

"Yeah. In our bed and… God, I can't believe I'm telling you this, but…I caught him." Her voice turned bitter and shaky. "He was fucking her from behind, and he said he was going to… Swear not to be mad?"

"Why would I be mad? I had nothing to do with any of this."

"Just swear."

"Okay." Boone leaned back and draped a casual

arm around the bench, not quite touching her shoulders. Just being this close to her was making his dick thump against his pants. "I swear."

"He was telling her he was going to fuck her like a werebear, which doesn't even make any sense, because he is anti-shifter, but she was screaming for him to, and when I walked in, I got a perfect shot of his ass and his spread legs. His perfectly shaved chode now visits my nightmares. I saw his balls clench as he emptied himself into this woman on our bed. And then he turned around like, *hey honey, I thought you were working late tonight*, like we were having a normal conversation and he wasn't buried balls deep in that woman. And then the woman he was banging—the one still attached to his dick— turned around with this pouty face and called Eddie a liar, and I thought for a second that he'd told her he was single, and for a tiny moment, I didn't hate her, but then she said that Eddie was a liar because he'd told her I was ugly, and I wasn't 'half bad.' And then I told him to get out, but he kicked me out instead, and I've been living in one of the condos trying to figure out what to do with myself. And I shouldn't miss him, and I don't miss him per say, but I miss being the other half of something. I'm rambling."

Boone ate another chocolate to wash away the vision of that prick's balls clenching as she'd described. He had the overwhelming urge to rake a claw down Eddie's soft human stomach until his guts fell out, but Cora didn't need to hear the bloody plans his inner monster was currently hatching. Clearly, a strong woman like Cora Wright didn't need him to avenge her.

"That was too much information," she said in a voice that sang of bone-deep regret.

"No, it was just enough," he lied. Humans couldn't hear dishonesty like he could. "Have you told anybody anyone else all of those...details?"

"You look really grossed out. No, only you."

Well that perked him right up and made his innards glow like a friggin' fiery s'more marshmallow. Damn, he made a pathetic monster around Cora. "Eddie's an idiot. You know that, right?"

"Yeah, I know. It's just hard to not feel like it was my fault somehow. Like"—her voice dipped to a quavering whisper—"maybe I wasn't good enough."

"I can tell you right now, that isn't it. Speaking as your friend—"

"Stranger," she corrected.

"And as a man—"

"Bear shifter."

"I can say with full certainty that Eddie is a sniveling taint-weevil who enjoys feeling powerful by treating women like they are beneath him. And also, werebears don't just fuck from behind, so he's obviously shite at animal science as well."

Cora's face had dipped into a relieved smile, but at his final revelation, the grin faded off her face completely. "Really?"

"Not that I haven't before, but I enjoy all positions." He frowned and amended, "Most positions."

"I bet you do. You have quite the reputation around town, Boone Keller."

"Do I?"

"Oh, yes." She cocked an eyebrow seriously, but her smile gave her away. "I read a picket sign about you. Riddled with animal STDs and fleas, it hinted."

A snort blasted up his throat as he tried not to laugh. "No to fleas, and we don't get STDs, so clearly, the picketer was another sadly misinformed human. Now that you know, you can call bullshit on them next time you pass by."

She giggled, and the easy sound cast away the chill and warmed him from his guts out.

"You said taint-weevil," she said, pink, glossy lips shining in the morning light. He wanted to suck them to see if they tasted as good as they looked.

"And I meant it."

"I don't even know what that means."

"I'll draw you a picture someday."

"He never bought me flowers," she said suddenly, her lips pursing as if she tasted something sour in those words. "I should've known that was a bad sign. And I get it. Some girls don't want flowers, but I asked for them. Often. He didn't like saying the L word, so I thought if he bought me flowers, it would be proof he cared. He just wouldn't buy me any. Not even cheap ones, not ever."

Her back brushed the inside of his elbow he had draped behind her, and his heartbeat stuttered in his chest. "You want me to eat him?"

There it was, that beautiful smile. "Do you actually do that to people you don't like?"

No, he shot them with sniper rifles or sicced dragons on them. Cora was good to the bone and didn't need to hear about what he'd done to keep the Breck Crew safe, though. "I don't have a taste for human flesh."

"I'm glad you didn't catch those kids who taped you," she said softly. "It would've brought you more trouble."

Unease slithered through his middle, and he dragged his gaze back to the red brick wall in front of them. He'd gone through hell since that tape had released a few days ago. From Cody and from some of the shifter-opposed in town. That little gem probably would've overturned the vote for them to go back to work as firefighters if it had come out a week earlier. "Out of all the people who have watched that video," he murmured low, "I wish you hadn't seen it."

"What were you dreaming of?"

Nope, he definitely wasn't telling Cora he'd been dreaming of her death. "Fishing and raspberry patches and jars of half-eaten honey."

She scrunched up her adorable nose and huffed a soft laugh, then shook her head. "I imagine it's hard to open up to people when you've had to hide for so long."

"Not really." More lies. "I just don't have any nut-clenching stories to share with virtual strangers."

Cora swatted him and laughed. "You think you're traumatized by that visual? I saw it with my own poor eyeballs. I'll never get that vision out of my head. Hey," she said, pulling her sunglasses from her face and swinging her open gaze to him. Her eyes were blue around the edges and brown in the middle, making them look gold in the saturated sunlight. "Thank you for this. You didn't have to take the time to talk to me, but I actually feel a lot better."

"Sure. Anytime you have horrifying, mind-damaging stories to tell, you know who to come to."

Cora grabbed her middle and giggled until her eyes crinkled at the corners. "I am kind of sorry."

"Kind of? I'm going to have nightmares and uncontrollable shifts for weeks."

"Please. Half-eaten jars of honey sound much more terrifying." She popped a chocolate-covered cherry into her mouth and her eyes went wide. "These are orgasmic."

Boone huffed a laugh and stood. "All right, stranger friend. I have to go find my crew and get back to work. Gage has probably bought out the entire candy shop by now. He has a ridiculous sweet tooth."

"See," she said, standing and dusting off her backside. "That is the kind of stuff the public needs to know. It humanizes you."

Boone slowed his long strides so she could keep up beside him. Damn, she was cute, and to stop his fingers from itching to touch hers, he linked his hands behind his head. "Cody says we need a publicist. He gave me a stack of applications last week and told me to pick one, but none of them seem the right fit for my crew."

"A publicist would help, but I agree. You need someone you can trust with your image. How people perceive you is everything right now, and you shifters are going to have to build from the ground up. I can ask around and see if I can track down a couple of options for you. I have a lot of connections at the station."

"I'd appreciate it. I wouldn't mind you interviewing my family either, if you ever get the time."

"You'd give me an exclusive interview?"

"Yeah. It's something Cody has brought up a few times already."

"All right, gimme." She fluttered her fingers. "Let me see your phone."

He pulled it from his back pocket and handed it over. Cora punched in her number and hit the call button. When her phone rang, she pulled it from her purse and saved his contact. "Since we're now friends, we should have each other's numbers anyway, in case I ever think of another wildly inappropriate story to tell you. And you, Mr. Keller," she said, handing him back his phone, "are the first man I've given my number to since I met Eddie. Call me when you're ready to set up that interview." Cora waved and walked away.

And as he watched her leave, phone clutched in his hand, he inhaled deeply and reveled in the silence.

For the first time in months, his inner bear wasn't snarling to escape his skin.

FOUR

"Tish, I don't know. I just feel better. Lighter without him now. It was so heavy that first week, but now I feel freer than I've felt in a long time."

Tish, the station's hair stylist, pulled at the bright pink tress of hair Cora had dyed last night. "Is that freedom where this came from?"

Sheepishly, she smiled. "I know it seems weird, but Eddie hated spontaneity, and I've always wanted to rock a little peekaboo color, and I don't know. Last night it was just nice to do something I wanted. Something that made me feel good."

"Well, thank you for putting it some place I can pin it out of view from the cameras. I don't know how ready the public is for your wild, spontaneous hairdo," Tish said, gray eyes sparkling. "I'm happy for you, girl. Whatever you're doing to get over that pinhead, Eddie, keep right on, because I've noticed a big change in you over the past couple of weeks, and it's been kind of awesome to watch."

In her reflection in the giant wall mirror that hung in the hair and make-up room, Cora's expression faltered. Boone had been the one to cause the stirrings of these changes, but he hadn't called or made contact in any way over the past two weeks. It was as if he'd disappeared into thin air. She'd felt a strong connection, friendship or whatever, with him, but he'd obviously bolted.

"Delivery for Cora Wright," a man with a giant bouquet of pink and orange roses said. The thing was so big, it covered his torso, and the man wasn't slender.

"For me?" she asked, baffled.

"Yes, ma'am. I'll set it right here. The card is in the middle. You two have a nice day." The delivery man settled the flowers on the table, fluffed the stems once, then bustled back out the door.

Slowly, she leaned forward and plucked the card from the bouquet. Inside the tiny envelop was a yellow sheet of paper.

Because a woman like you deserves flowers, even if they are from a friend.

At the bottom of the card, there was a scribbled cartoon of a cheerful looking ball sack and taint with a little smiley face and bug legs. It was labeled *taint-weevil.*

"Ha!" she laughed louder than she'd meant to. She couldn't help her face-splitting grin as she read and re-read the card.

Boone had sent her flowers, but more importantly than that...he'd listened.

"Five minutes, the producer said into the open doorway as he bustled by.

No time to call Boone now, but her stomach did curious flip-flops when she thought about talking to him after the show. *Focus.* She needed to calm down and trample the giddy feeling in her middle before she flubbed her lines and put Brandon and Deanna on the spot for an impromptu save-Cora-from-humiliating-herself-on-television scene. Like Eddie, her co-workers did not enjoy spontaneity. *Eddie.* Another wave of happiness washed over her as she realized the thought of him didn't bow her over anymore, and hadn't for days. In fact, she didn't feel anything but anger toward him now. And pity. He was destined to lead a sad and lonely life, never knowing how to give his heart to someone and have it protected. He would always be a rat, and she pitied anyone who ended up with him.

And Boone...sure, he'd put her squarely in the friend-zone with his note, but she was happy to be there.

He'd sent her flowers, her first ever, and Cora was suddenly glad Eddie hadn't ever listened.

****

It was late, past eleven, and Cora was dog tired as she always was after doing the late night news in studio. It wasn't her favorite part of the job. Any day of the week, she preferred to be sent out on assignment to cover events hosted by the town. It was a small station that catered only to the local area, so the staff was minimal, and most of them floated between multiple jobs that Mark, the producer, assigned them to.

She fought the urge to pull off her peep-toe pumps and walk barefoot the rest of the way to her car. All she wanted to do was get behind the wheel, lock the door, and call Boone to thank him for...well...for bringing her back to life.

She started hard when she saw a towering, shadowy figure leaned up against her car. Heart threatening to leap from her throat, she pulled an oversize serrated pocket knife from her purse and flipped it open with a practiced flick of her wrist.

"Put your knife away, woman. I'm not here to mug you."

Boone's familiar deep timbre settled her into a heaving sigh. "You scared the devil out of me."

"I can tell. You looked ready to gut me." His words were laced with frank approval, so she squared her shoulders and slipped the knife back inside the hidden pocket, feeling a lot safer with a scary-looking bear shifter than when she'd left the building alone. She didn't know why she was so certain, but Boone wouldn't let anyone mess with her.

Cora hefted up the giant vase of flowers. "Some hunky friend of mine sent me these," she teased. "Do you like them?"

Boone rocked his weight off her car and licked his lips as he approached. "I do. Did you like the cartoon?"

"I laughed entirely too loud, and my hairdresser made me explain. I'll keep the note forever." She had a spot already picked out for it in the bottom of her underwear drawer where she kept meaningful birthday cards from Grandma Ruth and tiny trinkets she'd collected over the years.

He chuckled, the sound low and alluring as he took the floral burden from her hands.

Tonight he was dressed down. Gray V-neck thermal sweater that clung to his wide shoulders just right, sleeves pushed up enough to let those sexy curls of ink peek out from underneath, leather necklace that dipped beneath his collar, medium wash jeans with designer holes at the knees and dark, scuffed work boots. His hair was loose tonight and a strand fell in front of his face and lifted slightly in the breeze. She wished she could touch it to see if it was as soft as it looked. The epitome of masculine beauty, dangerous and alluring all at once.

"Hey, Boone?" she said, dragging her gaze to the soft, blond day-old scruff on his chiseled jaw. "I just wanted to thank you for the flowers. I know it probably doesn't seem like a big deal to a man, but it was a pretty cool moment for me."

He shot her a thoughtful glance as she unlocked her Outback, then he opened the door and strapped the vase to the passenger seat with the seatbelt. With an explosive sigh, he stood, shrugging against the material of his shirt like it was constraining him. "I don't date."

"Okay."

"I mean, I'm not interested in you like that."

Her heart dropped to her toes, but she straightened her spine and lifted her chin. "Good, because I don't like you like that either. You're hideous." A smile crept across her lips, but she stifled it and held his gaze.

"Feisty," he accused.

"Rude," she dished back.

"What's this?" he asked, frowning at her hair.

Her breath caught as he reached beneath her curled tresses and touched at the pin that held her pink hair in place. A slow smile transformed his face as he pulled it loose.

"Do you like it?" she asked on a breath, rocked off her axis by how much his answer mattered.

"Yeah, I like it. When did you do it?"

"Last night. Eddie wouldn't have approved, and I felt like doing something that made me feel...pretty."

"Pretty fuckin' sexy and job well done. If I was into stuff like that. Which I'm not, because—"

"We're just friends, and you don't date. I get it. So why are you here, Boone Keller, if not to woo me?"

"I'm taking you out. To a bar with other people, so it's not a date or anything. It's a get-together." He ran his hands through his hair and muttered a curse, then leveled her a narrow-eyed look. "I had a shit day and I wanted to cut loose, and you seem like you'd be fun to drink with. Friend."

"I'm extremely fun to drink with, *friend*."

"You know that bar off of Lincoln?"

"Yeah, but it'll be crawling with tourists, bear-shifter man. You ready to sign autographs and fend off groupies?"

"They have cheap shots and fifty cent pool tonight."

"Touché. Well worth the oglers. I'm in, but not dressed like this. Meet you there?" Why did the thought of cutting this conversation short make her want to step closer to him? She snuggled deeper into her jacket and forced her feet to stay planted like

Cypress roots.

"Sure." He reached out and tugged the curl she'd dyed. "See you there, Trouble."

Her cheeks warmed as he walked away, and she pressed her cold knuckles against the flush there to cool her face. She liked that pet name. He cast her a quick glance before hopping into an old, rusted-out, beat-up clunker Chevy. It had probably been blue at some point if the fine strips of remaining paint were anything to go by. For some reason, it struck her as so...Boone. Sure, he could probably afford nicer on his fireman's salary, but the man seemed to harbor a quiet loyalty that stretched from his crew to his ride. He'd probably kept the thing running for years.

As dangerous as it was to think of him in any light bar friendship, there was nothing sexier on this earth than a loyal man.

FIVE

The skintight little black dress and sky-high heels Cora had chosen for beer pong night at a local tavern had seemed like a good idea until she made it about two blocks in the cold autumn air. By block three, she was covered in gooseflesh, shivering, and sporting twin blisters on the backs of her ankles, but Grandma Ruth didn't *raise no complainer*, as she'd often told Cora when growing up under her roof. So on she marched, clutching her purse, hoping this wasn't some sort of prank and Boone wasn't going to stand her up.

She'd primped for him.

There it was, the thought out in the universe. Was it annoying that she wanted him to look at her as more than a friend? Yes. Hell yes! He'd made it clear he wasn't into her like that, but gosh dang it, Boone was clamp-that-mouth-shut-wipe-that-drool sexy, and it wasn't fair that she was the only one who had to donkey kick her hormones back below magma-heat levels around him. He should be affected by her too, hence the dress.

The nerves kicked in as she turned onto Lincoln Avenue. She gripped her purse to steady one of her shaking hands and tugged self-consciously at the hem of her dress as she turned up the walkway to the bar, heels clip-clopping over the cement. The bar was rustic and had been around for a hundred years, at least. It had been a shop during the mining days when Breckenridge first started booming. Dark wood siding around the exterior with cream-colored trim, the bar was a quaint mix of mountain cabin and cozy Victorian abode with a wraparound front porch and old-fashioned lanterns in the windows. Rock music blared from inside as she reached for the door handle.

She could do this. It was just Boone, her friend, and a bunch of locals and tourists, and after a shot or two of cheap tequila, she'd be just fine.

What was wrong with her? She didn't even get this nervous before going on-air. *Stop it. You're okay. You're a strong-ass, independent woman, and he's just a man. A sexy, intimidating, wild man who is probably a thief of hearts and a demon in the sack, but still—just a man.*

With a steadying breath, she hesitated, then pulled open the door. Inside, the bar was dim, illuminated in gold by the hanging pendant lights. Scattered everywhere were dark wooden tables and mismatched chairs. The murmur of the full bar warred with the volume of the music, but all that died to nothing when her gaze landed on Boone.

He was leaned back on a barstool, talking to Dade Keller, his younger brother. Rolled sleeves on his tight gray sweater showed off the ink on his arms as he rested his elbows behind him, and his abs flexed against the thin material of his shirt as he laughed low and shook his head at something his younger brother said to him. But when his nostrils flared and his eyes tracked to her, he stilled and the smile faded from his lips.

She stood frozen there, prey under a predator's gaze. Heart-thumping, pulse roaring in her ears. She swallowed hard at his hungry stare as he dipped his attention to her legs, then raked back up her body. Pretend all he wanted, but with a look like that, Boone wanted her on some base level as much as she wanted him.

With every second he held her trapped in his gaze, her crush on him grew, pulsing against her insides, making it hard to breathe, hard to move.

A shadow covered her. A man with shoulders the width of a semi stepped in front of her, breaking Boone's spell and allowing her a trembling breath of relief.

"Hey, you're that lady from the news. I knew it was you. Derek," the man called with a big grin peeking out from beneath his full beard, "I told you, it's really her." A trio of guys at a pool table nodded and waved, so she smiled politely back.

"Hey, can I get your autograph? My lady and I watch you all the time."

"Of course," she said, cheeks burning.

"My name's Jack." He offered his hand, then pumped hers in a bone-rattling handshake.

"Cora," she said with a giggle. "Nice to meet you, Jack. You have anything for me to sign? I have a pen in my purse, but no paper."

Jack frowned thoughtfully and scanned the immediate area, then snatched a discarded bar receipt from a nearby chair. He unrumpled it and handed it to her. Leaning over a tall, circular table, she signed it *To my bar buddy, Jack*, then scribbled her name and handed it back.

"Hey, thanks Cora. My lady, Jenny is her name, she's not going to believe she missed meeting you tonight. She wanted to let me have a guy's night. She's real sweet like that. Hey, can I buy you a drink? Strictly as a friend who is in a happy, healthy relationship with someone else. Just as a thank you."

Cora opened up her mouth to say he didn't have to go to the trouble, but a beer appeared in front of her, held by one oversize hand with ink curled up to the edge of a storm-gray sweater sleeve.

"Sorry, man. I've already got this one," Boone said with an easy smile. "You want to get the next one?"

Cora canted her head and smiled as she accepted the drink. He wasn't being mean to Jack or acting jealous and standoffish like Eddie would've done. Here was a man completely at ease with his place in the world. That, or he really wasn't jealous because they were just friends. Her smile dipped, so she covered it by taking a swig of her beer.

"Hey, you're one of those bear people from on the news!" Jack said. "Derek!" Jack gripped Boone's shoulder and shook him slowly like he was a long lost friend. "It's one of those bear people! In this bar. Drinking with us!"

Derek was a short man with big muscles pushing against his flannel shirt. His dark eyes hardened when he looked up from his game of pool and glared at Boone. He didn't wave to Boone like he'd waved to Cora.

"What's your problem, man?" Jack asked.

"Don't care about no fuckin' bears, Jack." Derek spat the word *bears* with vitriol.

"Whatever. Barkeep!" Jack called out, diverting his attention to the bar in back. "Put their next drinks on my tab. We've got bona fide famous people in here tonight."

"I sure appreciate it," Boone said, shaking his hand. "We'll see ya."

"Yeah," Jack said in a dreamy voice. "Oh, can I get a picture with you two so I can show my lady I wasn't just drunk and making this up?"

Cora laughed and said, "Sure."

She and Boone flanked him as he pulled his phone out, and she smiled her best news reporter grin as Jack gave a thumbs-up sign and took a selfie of all of them.

Boone clapped him on the shoulder and told Jack how nice it was to meet him, then pressed his palm on the lowest point of Cora's back and gently guided her to a table in the back corner of the bar.

Leaning down, he murmured, "You look beautiful." He cleared his throat once, as if he'd remembered himself and amended, "but that dress doesn't make any damned sense in a place like this."

"I live in a condo with about a quarter of my wardrobe. Take what you can get, Keller."

He halted and narrowed his eyes, then leaned down and whispered in her ear, "I don't like you calling me by my last name."

"Why not, friend?" She'd meant for the words to come out strong and forceful, but they came out unsteady and breathy instead. His lips were so close to her ear, and he wasn't pulling away. Her knees wobbled.

"My handler used to call me by my last name." He pulled her sensitive earlobe between his teeth and left them there for a moment, grazing her skin. He bit down gently before he released her, causing her sex to pulse once between her legs.

Afraid her knees were really going to give out, she clutched his arm and leaned forward. "What is a handler?" she asked on a shaky breath.

Boone's arm flexed to steel under her palm, and he eased back. His eyes had gone cold and closed down, ice blue where moments before they'd been warm. "Nothing you need to concern yourself with. Come on. I want to you meet some people. And don't freak out or read anything into meeting my family. You need to get to know them for the interviews."

Right. Put in her place again, so she wouldn't get the wrong idea after he'd sucked on her ear in the middle of a crowded bar and soaked her panties. Oaf. Irritated, she pushed off him and took a long swig of her beer as she approached the back where some of the Breck Crew were hanging out. She didn't need Boone to make introductions if he was going to be a jerk about this. Hot and cold, like a faucet with a faulty water heater, that was Boone, and she didn't like games. Never had.

She marched past the beer pong tournament and stuffed longhorn steer heads on the wall. Past the counter where the bartender nodded his head and smiled a greeting. Past the hallway to the restrooms and the giant Bud Light signs hanging down from the exposed beam ceilings like tapestries.

She nearly stomped her clacking high heels up until the point where Dade Keller turned around, all cropped blond hair, intense blue eyes like his brother, and a knowing smile she had no clue what to do with. When, one by one, Dade, Cody, Rory, and Quinn noticed her approach, she got a funny feeling of being trapped, as if she'd walked into a den of sleeping lions.

"H-hi." Her professional composure out the window, the pressure of meeting Boone's family face-to-face suddenly seemed overwhelming. Sure, she'd been there when the bears had turned Quinn and come out to the public, and she'd been there at the conference where the Breck Crew tried to calm the world about their existence. But they weren't just some bear shifters she wanted to score an interview with. They were important to Boone. Great hairy balls, why did this suddenly matter so much to her? "Where's the other one? The big one? Oldest? With the cubs. Gage?" She cleared her throat as her cheeks turned to molten lava. This was going swimmingly well.

"Gage," Boone said from beside her, giving her the strangest look, "is at the station tonight. His mate, Leah, and my ma are watching the cubs so we could all get a night out together."

"You have cubs?"

Why was he staring at her like she'd lost her mind?

"Oh, you mean Cody's cub, Aaron. I said that right, right? Humans call them cubs, too? Shit. Shoot." Cora pursed her lips and blinked hard. "I swear, your interviews will go much smoother. Boone did tell you about them?"

Cody, alpha of the Breck Crew, was grinning now, and her embarrassment went bone deep. She was screwing everything up, and this wasn't like her! She was the calm one under pressure. It was Boone's fault for doing that sexy thing to her ear, then sending her to meet his family. Double oaf.

"He told us, and I think it's a good idea. We could

use some good PR, especially after today."

"Why? What happened today?" Cora looked from Cody to Dade to Boone, whose eyes went vacant as he shut down completely on her. How was it so easy for him to flip the switch like that?

"It's really nice to meet you," Quinn said, standing up from the large, round table and offering her hand. She looked much better than the last time Cora had seen her at the town hall when she'd defended the Breck Crew in front of a line of national news crews. She had color in her fair cheeks, and her auburn hair was shinier and longer. Fear didn't live in her gray-sky eyes anymore. She'd grown stronger over the last couple of months, though how much of that was from healing her injuries, or how much was from the new bear inside of her, Cora hadn't a guess.

Cora shook her hand with a grateful sigh that the woman had saved her from rambling further.

"It's nice to finally talk to you in person," Rory, Cody's fiery red-headed mate said with a bright smile. "You've kind of been circling our family as we've come out, and I just wanted to let you know that your support has meant a lot to our crew. You've been rallying people."

"You've seen the website?" Now Cora was really blushing. She'd created the site to host the facts she'd researched, the video of their coming out, and the filming at the town hall where the crew had spoken publicly for the first time. But honestly, since the move to the condo, she hadn't moderated it much.

"Yeah, we've all popped onto the forums to answer questions over the past couple of days," Quinn said. "We figured it was a good place to start to dispel the rampant rumors. It is currently the most shifter-positive site we've been able to find on the web, so thank you for setting that up."

"Sorry about the trolls," Cora said, taking an offered seat between the two women. "I try to limit the hate posts, but I haven't been on there much in the last few weeks. Life got...complicated." Meaning Eddie-The-Cheating-Butt-Face had made her life complicated, and the internet at the condo was patchy.

Cody leaned forward, steely gaze steady, honesty pooling in his eyes when he said, "Well, you have proven to be one of our best allies over the past couple of months. You were the one who told me to stop talking to the public after Dade Changed Quinn, when our emotions were all running high, and I know you did that to protect my crew. And you didn't have to do that. You must've been shocked along with the rest of the public when Quinn Turned in front of everyone."

"Yeah, I was definitely there with my cameraman to report on the veterinary clinic fire, not hide behind a fire engine from a bunch of grizzly-people."

"Bear shifters," Boone said softly, settling into a chair across the table from her. "Say it."

"Bear shifters," she repeated in a quiet voice. The bar was loud, but she knew how good their hearing was.

Boone nodded slowly, his eyes thoughtful, as if he'd enjoyed the way she said what he was. A chill brushed up her spine. "I think I need another drink." Something stronger, like rotgut whiskey or absinth.

"I got you," Boone said in a deep, rumbly voice that brushed over her skin with the promise that he did.

After he stood and sauntered over to the bar, Cora chugged the rest of her beer and gave into the Keller boys goading her into a game of darts. She sucked at darts, but after Quinn sank the first one deep into the wall outside the target, Cora felt better. At least she could make it into the outer ring of the circle.

Three turns, and Boone was back with a tray of amber-colored shots. He handed her the first, his eyes intent on hers, daring her to turn it down. Not one to shy away from a challenge, she took it from his hand, but murmured, "Keller, I have a public image to maintain, just like you do."

His eyes narrowed at the surname, but she was going to push it until he explained what a handler was. As the others gathered around the table, she sniffed at the shot glass. Whiskey if the burn in her nose was spot on. She didn't know why, but she was glad Boone hadn't ordered her a panty-dropper fruity shot and, instead, had trusted her to keep up with him and his family.

"To Cora, the Breck Crew's truest friend," Boone said.

Deep ache bloomed in her chest, but she ignored his attempt to remind her where she ranked here— outsider, not family, not crew—*other*. She gave him a stiff smile and clicked the bottom of the tiny glass on the table with the rest of them, then downed it and winced at the burn of the scorching liquor.

She laughed as Dade gave her a high-five. Quinn complained loudly at Boone's tastes in shots, but she was grinning like she was having the best time of her life. Snatching the darts from Cody's hand, Rory took her turn at the board while Dade made his way to the bar, probably for more shots.

"You smell different," Boone said from so close behind her, she could feel his warmth spreading across her shoulder blades.

"Oh? Can you smell irritation?"

"Is that what that is? Mmm," he murmured. "I thought it was arousal."

"Stop sniffing me," she said, spinning and smacking him soundly on the arm.

Boone's blond brows shot up. "Do that again?"

The first tingles of a good buzz were spreading through her lips, a sure sign she should slow it down on the booze. "No."

"Do it."

Admittedly, it did feel good to smack him, so she did it again. Boone laughed a disbelieving sound and looked down. Cora followed his gaze to the seam of his pants, which seemed to be constraining a rather sizable dick. Long and thick and definitely hard.

"Boone Keller, did you just get a boner?"

"No one's ever slapped me like that before."

"What?" Cora lowered her voice as she tried to stop the laughter that bubbled up the back of her throat. "Don't be weird."

He leaned on locked arms on the table and stared at her, grinning.

"Boone Festus Keller, make it go away. People have camera phones." God, she couldn't stop giggling. "I just made up your middle name, by the way."

"I could tell. It's Leland. Family name. All my brothers' middle names are the same." He looked down at his crotch again with a big dumb grin. "I don't give a shit about camera phones."

"You should."

"Feel it. Woman, you got me really hard."

"Stop it."

"I'm serious." He leaned forward and dared her, "Feel my dick."

"Boone, I already told you I have an image to maintain. I'm not going to touch your dick in public."

"In public," he repeated.

"Or anywhere else," she said, lifting her chin

primly. "I'm unaffected by you."

"Oh yeah? You want me to take you into that hallway over there and show you just how affected by me you can be?"

"I don't even know what that means." Her words were breathy and faint now.

Boone leaned over and took another shot from a tray Dade was carrying. "You want?"

"More whiskey? I don't want to steal yours."

"I'm cutting myself off before I get us both into more trouble than we need tonight."

Cora narrowed her eyes so hard, Boone's crooked grin went blurry. She snatched the shot from his hand, sloshing just a drop, then tipped it up and gulped it down. With a screw-you arch to her brow, she set the empty back on the table. "I don't know what that means either, Boone Leland Keller." Oh, her words were beginning to slur now.

Boone straightened his spine with his arms crossed over his chest, indecision warring over his features as his gaze dipped to her mouth. Slowly, he leaned forward and brushed his lips against hers. Shocked to her core, Cora went rigid. Boone's fingertips brushed softly up her bare arm, over her collar bone, up her neck, where he cupped her with his warm hand. His lips softened and parted against hers, and his tongue brushed the closed seam of her mouth. Angling his head, he moved his frame closer, making her feel all warm and safe, as if they were the only ones in the room. With a moan, she opened slightly for him, allowing him to taste her as her belly filled with a tingling sensation that nearly locked her legs. Boone eased back, but leaned into her again with a sexy pluck of her lips, then leaned back again. With a wicked grin, he pulled her arms around his neck, then wrapped her up in a strong embrace and lowered his lips beside her ear.

"If I took you in that hallway, slid that sexy little dress up your thighs, and pulled your soaking panties to the side. If I slid my finger in you and let you fuck my hand, would you be affected by me then?"

Cora let off a shuddering, incomprehensible noise. "Yes. Please?" The hallway suddenly sounded like the happiest place on earth.

Boone's lips skimmed the oversensitive skin on her neck. He smiled against her skin there. "You're tipsy, and fooling around while drinking isn't my move."

"You gave me the shots." She was pouting.

"Yeah," he said, backing away. He sauntered over to the dartboard and said over his shoulder, "And now we're both safe from each other."

Cora glared at his stupid, sexy head and leaned heavily on the table beside her. Boone, that ass, had drawn her inner goddess from her, got her revved up hotter than a muscle car, and then batted her away like a cat toying with a mouse. The hormone dump to her system left her shaky and weak, and her nerve endings between her legs were firing double-time. Three strokes, and he could've had her.

Pissed at being teased, she grabbed her purse and swallowed down the rampant disappointment spiraling through her middle.

"Hey," Dade called, "you aren't leaving, are you?"

She cast a glance over her shoulder and shook her head. "I just need a minute." Stupid voice as it cracked with emotion. Boone was too deep in her head. It wasn't Boone the animal that was dangerous to her. It was Boone the man who was conjuring the ability to wreck her completely.

The bathroom was one of those lockable, single-room numbers, thank goodness, because she was in serious jeopardy of crying. Boone had done that. Normally, she was the happiest drunk on the planet, yet here she was feeling toyed with and emotional.

She didn't have to use the restroom, but she couldn't go back out there until she was in complete control of her mental faculties again, so she checked her email on her phone. Nothing would settle her raging hormones faster than work messages from her producer. She had contacts all over the area, and three had sent her tips on news stories today. The first two were easy to ignore, a cat had a two-headed kitten and the other was a liquor store burglary that went wrong. The last, however, caught her attention with the title of the email.

Your Bears Lost a Person Today.

Frowning as a heaviness filled the pit of her stomach, she opened the email and read it as fast as her eyes could scan the words. House fire…Fairplay, Colorado…one woman rescued, husband lost to the blaze…all Kellers at the scene…

That's why Boone had said he'd had a shit day. That's why Cody had mentioned they needed good PR after a day like today. A failed rescue, and Boone hadn't once mentioned it. That's how much she meant to him. Not enough to share a single real thing about himself.

"Cora, let me in," Boone said from the other side.

Horrified, she shoved her phone back into her purse. "Fuck off, *Keller*."

"Look, I'm sorry. I shouldn't have kissed you. Please, just let me in."

"I'm taking a piss."

"No, you aren't. I can hear everything, remember? No peeing, only sniffling, and now I feel like a total dick."

Ding, ding, ding. Winner, winner, werebear dinner.

Cora locked her arms on the sink and glared at her reflection in the mirror. Damn, she'd dressed up for this. Shaking her head, she wiped her damp lashes with a paper towel, mentally patted herself on the back that no tears actually fell for that triple oaf. Determined to blow past him, she threw open the door.

"No, wait," he drawled out, easing her back into the bathroom. "Talk to me."

"Okay," she said as he turned and locked the door behind him. "You have a filthy mouth. Which I realize I like, but you play head games with me, and I hate it. Hate. It. My ex cheated on me, made me feel like crap, and dragged my self-esteem through the mud. Now the guy I'm interested in can't stay interested in me back for more than thirty seconds. I haven't ever had an orgasm with a man, and I know that's too much information, but there it is. And you almost draw one from me just by kissing me, but then you shut me down if I react, and dammit, I'm tired of being shut down, Boone." A sob lodged in her throat, but she stomped her heel hard onto the tile floor and bit her lip to stop it from emerging. Boone did not deserve to see her break down. "If you don't want me, don't tease me. You're the one always putting me in the stupid friend-zone, and I get it. You aren't ready for a relationship, and not one with me. Fine. Great. Fan-fuckin'-tastic, but don't play with me anymore. And if you can't help yourself, or if you are one of those arrogant pricks who needs a woman they aren't interested in to fawn all over him, then I don't think we should be friends anymore. I've done that relationship before, remember? I got really hurt."

Boone heaved a sigh and leaned back against the paper towel dispenser with his arms crossed over his chest. "I'm not trying to hurt you."

"Then what are we doing? This," she said, pointing back and forth between them, "feels like more than friendship." Her voice dipped lower as she rested her back against the opposite wall. "I don't think that friends is working for me."

Boone ran his hands through his hair. His eyes had lightened to a strange color, and the smile he'd donned earlier was nowhere to be seen now. "Friends is all I can do, Cora. It's that or nothing."

She swallowed the heartache down. "Friends actually share important parts of their lives."

Boone canted his head slightly, his arms flexing as he crossed them harder over his chest. "I don't understand."

"Don't worry, Boone. I'm not asking you anything about your bear shifter shit. I just got an email that told me about the fire today. I have to report this stuff in the news. You remember that, right? Were you just going to wait until I found out about it at work tomorrow? When I was going to have to report on the fire that you failed to mention, even though we hung out the whole night before?"

"There's nothing to say." His voice was soft and dangerous with the edge of a growl she'd never heard before. His eyes had lightened further to a green-gold color.

She nodded slowly. "Of course there's not. I don't want to do this anymore. Thank you for the flowers. That was really nice of you, but we don't feel the same way about each other, and I like to think I'm smart enough to learn from my mistakes. Excuse me," she whispered, opening the door beside him.

Cora walked away from him, out the door without another word. She said her goodbyes and nice-to-meet-yous to the others in the Breck Crew and made her way out of the bar.

Tonight had started out so promising but had ended with such bitter disappointment.

"Buck up, girl," she whispered to herself as she made her way down the cold, empty street.

Grandma Ruth didn't raise no complainer.

SIX

Cora wrapped her arms around her middle a little tighter to ward off the cold. Her shoes dangled from two fingers, and her purse was clutched in the other as she made her way toward Main Street. Right about now, it was so frigid out, she was wishing her buzz hadn't worn off with that sobering conversation she had with Boone in the bathroom.

The rumbling sound of an old engine approached from behind her, but she ignored it and kept walking.

Boone's old truck slowed to a crawl beside her, but still, she kept up her pace.

"Cora, can we talk?" he asked out his open window.

"We already did that, and like I told you then, I

don't need any of this."

"Look, I've gone twenty-eight years without talking to anyone about my life. It's not easy to turn that off. If I mess up and say the wrong thing, my crew will pay for it. Will suffer for it. Hell, they could die from it. For chrissakes, Cora, you're a reporter."

"Yeah, and I'm also a loyal human being, Boone." She turned and faced his truck, furious at his lack of trust. "I've given you no reason not to trust me, but you still treat me like I'm going to sell you and your family out at any moment. Have I ever done anything to jeopardize your crew? I was the first to defend them, at the risk of my career. You know what? Forget it. I'm tired and cold, and I don't want to have this conversation anymore. I don't enjoy talking myself in circles. It makes me want to break things."

"At least let me give you a ride. If you don't, I swear I'll follow you the entire way home."

With a pathetically human-sounding growl, she stomped to the passenger's side and climbed in, then buckled her seatbelt. "Happy?"

"No," he said, reaching in the back seat of his truck. "I pissed you off, or hurt you, or both. I made you cry, so no, I'm not happy."

He pulled a jacket over her lap, one that smelled of him and the rich scent of animal fur. Then he turned the heat up to full blast and pulled over on the side of the road.

"What are you doing?"

"Telling you about my day."

Her chest heaved as she stared at him, waiting for the punchline to his joke.

"I was supposed to get off a long, forty-eight hour shift early this morning, but right when my brothers and I were about to head out, we got a call. It was a house fire in Fairplay, but when we got there, it had spread to the barn and surrounding woods as well. The wind had kicked up, and everything was so dry… Anyway, my crew rescued a woman from inside an upstairs bedroom. She was pretty banged up, burns on her arms and was having trouble breathing, but she kept saying she couldn't find Manny. 'I can't find Manny. My Manny is still in there somewhere.'" Boone swallowed audibly and gripped the steering wheel as he stared straight ahead. Easing his truck forward, he said, "She'd been taking a nap when the fire started, and she thought he was still in the house, but he wasn't. I know because my brothers and I almost burned turning that place upside down in that blaze looking for him. He was in the barn, trying to let their horses out of the stalls, I guess. Maybe he thought his wife was already gone, or he hadn't been able to get to her. We heard him screaming. We can hear everything, and he was burning. I ran out to the barn, and it felt like every step took a hundred years as Manny screamed and screamed. Sometimes with fires, we can't get in the building. We just physically can't if they are already engulfed. We were using the hoses and just dumping water, just drowning the fire, but we couldn't get to him. That used to be my biggest fear."

"What?"

"Burning alive on a call."

Cora clutched the material of his jacket across her lap as she thought about losing Boone that way, and of the fear he had to face every day. "What are you most afraid of now?"

Boone swung his gaze to her. "You."

A pair of headlights blinded her for an instant from behind Boone before his truck shattered inward. She screamed as Boone reacted instantly to the force of the crash, shielding her body with his as shards of glass exploded toward them. Spinning out, stomach dipping, dizziness, screeching tires and a second later, it was done as the truck rocked to a violent stop on the other side of the road.

"Oh my gosh," she chanted over and over as she looked up into Boone's wide, feral, gold-hued eyes.

"Shh," he said, smoothing her hair from her face and dipping his chin, leveling her a hard look. "Tell me if you're hurt."

Why was he whispering so softly? The adrenaline was doing something strange to her body. Maybe she was in shock. She shook so hard it rattled her bones, and her breath trembled as she tried to draw oxygen into her lungs and take stock of her body. Thank God, she'd put on her seatbelt. Thank God, Boone had been wearing his.

A raspy voice sounded over the quiet street through the broken window. "I just have to check and make sure they're expired. No, I did it just as planned. It'll look like an accident."

Cora slammed her trembling hand over her mouth to hold in the scared sounds lodged in her throat.

"Tell me fast," Boone said on a breath. "Are you

hurt?"

She shook her head, too afraid to speak. Someone had done this on purpose. The man in the other car had been trying to hurt Boone. No, he'd been trying to hurt both of them. He'd said he needed to make sure *they're* expired. The sound of crunching glass under heavy footfall blasted terror through her veins. Her breath came in short, panicked gasps, but Boone pulled her face back to him. He pressed his finger over his lips and went limp, palm slipping from her. He groaned a soft, pained sound. Was he hurt? His hand squeezed her leg hard. No. Just playing opossum.

She was already hunched and leaned against the window, so she closed her eyes and slid her hand into her purse. There wasn't time to call the police and tell them an address. She couldn't look around and see the street signs, and talking right now wasn't even an option, but her reporter instincts screamed there should be some record of what was going down. When her grasp landed on the cold plastic of her cell, she turned it on video from memory and slid it out slowly. Sticky warmth trickled down her face, but it didn't hurt yet. The adrenaline was making her numb.

She couldn't stop shaking! Her rattling body would blow their cover.

"Fuck," the man said.

God, she wanted to open her eyes. This was so much scarier not knowing what this monster looked like.

"They're still breathing. Nah, there's no cameras on this street. No houses either. I picked it carefully. Yeah, I said I'll take care of it, and I will. I'll call you when it's done."

The door creaked open. Boone's body jerked away from her, and unable to keep still a moment longer, Cora's eyes flew open, and a scream burst from her throat. Boone had the man's wrist in his hand and jerked it hard. A loud *pop* sounded and the man gritted his teeth and made an agonized yelp as a syringe dropped from his grip to the space on the seat between her and Boone.

The man was generic looking. Hair smoothed back into place, as if he'd combed it after the wreck. Smooth-shaven face, enraged coffee-colored eyes, and impeccable suit. No blood on his face at all, as if he'd been lucky enough to hit an airbag. He was also highly trained, which was evident in him blocking every punch Boone threw at him, despite an obviously broken wrist.

Boone was trapped by the seatbelt as he fought for their lives, and there wasn't enough room in the cab of his shredded truck to fully extend his arm to box the man. He slammed the attacker against the door so hard, it fell off and skidded across the street.

Lurching forward, Cora unbuckled Boone's seatbelt, and he slid out of the truck, feral gaze intent on the man doubled over on the ground. "You work for IESA?" Boone asked, voice gravelly and low.

The man scrambled to his feet and wiped the sleeve of his dark suit jacket across his bloody lip. An empty, echoing laugh escaped him as he raised his fists, ready for another row with Boone. His left one was already swelling and painful looking, but didn't seem to bother him.

Terrified, Cora stumbled from the truck. She swallowed a sob when she got a glance at the destroyed front end of Boone's ride. Fingers shaking, she had to try twice to dial 911, and when she got through, she spouted off the intersection and told the dispatcher she'd been in a car wreck and the other man was trying to kill them. When she looked up,

Boone and the man were locked in a battle that was just as graceful as it was deadly. They never stopped moving, dodging, hitting, blocking, side-stepping. When a hit connected, the sickening sound of fist slamming into muscle brought bile to the back of her throat.

"You stupid animal," the man growled at the sound of sirens in the distance. "You were the warning, you and your whore. The rest of your crew would've come back in line."

Something shiny slashed through the air, and Boone jerked back. The arcing tip of a syringe missed him by millimeters. When Boone cupped the man's neck and slammed him against the concrete, the needle launched from the man's hand and skittered across the ground, cracking against the curb, spilling its contents.

Cora pulled the knife from her purse and screamed Boone's name as she bolted for him. He turned in time for her to slide the handle of her closed knife against the palm of his hand. In one smooth motion, he flicked the blade open and pressed it against the man's neck just enough to nick him. Crimson trailed in a sickening line down his throat as Boone applied more pressure. "It doesn't matter if you'd succeeded tonight. My crew won't every *come back in line* again."

"Kill me, Keller," the man rasped through an empty smile. He stretched his neck up against the blade. "Do it. Show everyone what a monster you are."

Boone lifted his gaze to the sidewalk where four bystanders stood, watching with horror written all over their features.

"If you kill me, it won't matter. There will be someone new to take my place, but you already know that. We're going to eradicate your kind until you are nothing but a dim memory. You didn't play by our rules, and now there will be consequences. You thought coming out to the public made you safer? Look in those people's eyes. They hate you. Hate what you stand for. IESA was the only thing that could've kept you safe."

Boone huffed a breath and shook his head. He looked sick, listening to those words. "You made me and my family kill all those people, all those shifters. Their deaths are on you."

"You pulled the triggers."

"I *was* the trigger," Boone yelled, voice cracking with power. "IESA is the gun, the bullets...the intent to murder. I should kill you just to make the world a better place, but that's too easy. You deserve to rot in jail."

"Oh." The man shook his head and pouted out his lip. "Poor dumb monster. You've become careless off your leash. You and I both know I won't ever see the inside of a jail cell." His voice dipped to a whisper. "I'll be back for you, but first...I'll be back for her."

"No!" Boone yelled, his face contorting to something terrifying. His eyes blazed, and the tendons in his neck strained as his voice turned to a roar.

His wide shoulders heaved once as a massive blond grizzly exploded from him.

Flashing lights illuminated his fur—red, blue, red, blue.

The crack of metal on metal echoed as a police officer screamed, "Stand down!"

Boone's rage filled the air with a popping sensation, like a bolt of electricity, lifting the hairs on Cora's arm.

"Boone!" she screamed, tears burning her eyes.

His claw was lifted in the air, hovered over the man ready to end him, but at her voice, he went rigid and cast her a feral glance over his shoulder.

Cora clutched tighter to the cell phone, the one she'd been using to record the man's admission to guilt. Voice wavering, she whispered, "I need you."

Please let that seep through his foggy mind. If he did this, it would ruin everything. Any hope of the Breck Crew ever being accepted. It would maim any chance of her and Boone being together. It would ensure that he got hurt.

"Please," she begged, "let the police have him."

Boone slammed his giant paw down right next to the man's face. He winced away but Boone was done with him. Slowly, the heavily muscled grizzly backed off the cowering man, hate-filled eyes never leaving his.

With a grunt, Boone turned and headed for the tall trees that towered over the next street of buildings.

"Freeze!" the police said.

"No, wait!" Cora yelled to the officer she'd worked with many times when she broke stories. "Monroe, this man attacked us, wrecked our car and tried to kill us. Boone needs a minute to get control of his animal. I will call his alpha, and he'll come back and answer questions as soon as he is able."

"It's Boone Keller?" The dark-haired officer asked, gun trained at the bear's receding back.

"Yes. He was defending me."

"On your knees," the officer demanded as the attacker rolled upward. "Hands behind your head."

"You're going to let the bear get away?" the man asked, fury cracking in his tone.

"He isn't getting away. I know him, where he works and lives. He's a good man, and if Cora says he'll come back, he will. Cora, make that call and get Cody out here."

Cora stopped the video and bolted for the truck. Hopefully Boone's phone hadn't been ejected through the broken window. Last she'd seen, it was sitting in a cup holder on the console. God, she hoped she was right and Boone wasn't running. She'd made up that bit and hoped she sounded confident enough. Cody would know what to do.

She glanced at the door on the ground, shocked at the force Boone had used against the man, then searched the cab of the pickup. *Please be here.*

Boone's phone had been thrown to the floorboard on the passenger side. Holding it in her rattling hands, she scrolled through his contacts. Her fingers felt too big for the screen, and she had to try several times, but she finally dialed Cody.

He picked up on the second ring. "Hey, Boone."

"Cody?"

A beat of silence followed. "What's happened?"

Cora looked out toward where the flaxen-furred bear had disappeared from the halo of the streetlight. "Boone needs you."

SEVEN

Quinn rubbed Cora's arm as a paramedic checked her pupils once more and gave her the all-clear. She had a couple of lacerations to her cheek from the broken window glass, but they were so shallow, she hadn't even needed stitches. Boone had taken the brunt of the crash when he shielded her body with his and held her in an iron grip.

Rory approached with a sympathetic smile. "Monroe is taking the last of Boone's statement, but he said you're free to go."

She slid stiffly from the back of the ambulance. "I'm going to wait for him."

"We figured you would. We'll wait, too."

"What about your cub?" she asked Rory.

"Aaron is staying the night with Ma and his cousins tonight. It's no trouble to stay. Besides, Cody is calling a meeting."

"Oh." Cora floundered, unsure of where she stood with private crew affairs.

Cody stood some distance off, leaning against his truck beside Dade, but he arched his gaze to Cora and called, "You're in this now. The meeting involves you, too, if you're up for coming."

"Yeah," she murmured. "Where should I meet you?" Her words came out hollow with shock, but that was to be expected. She felt like she was floating in a dream. Or a nightmare.

Cody waved to the passing fire truck, and the oldest Keller brother, Gage, waved from behind the wheel. The fire department showed up about five minutes after she'd called 911 in case more help was needed.

"Once the wrecker finishes towing Boone's truck, you can ride with Rory and me to the station. Gage is on shift, but he needs to hear what really happened, too.

"But Boone is already telling the police what really happened."

Cody cocked an eyebrow and waited.

Right. He wanted to hear what really *really* happened. As in, the information Boone and his animal had been able to pick up that the police wouldn't know what to do with.

Quinn was running her hands through Cora's hair in a soothing rhythm. "Looks like Monroe is finished with Boone's statement."

Her heart clenched with worry as Boone shook the officer's hand and took an offered sheet of paper. He talked low to Monroe, folding the paperwork absently, then he turned his gaze toward her, as if he could feel her watching. She couldn't read Boone's expression at all. Closed off, for certain, but beyond that, she didn't see worry or pain, or even anger. He was shutting down again, and the ache in her chest bloomed wider.

There was no stiff limp in his gait as he sauntered toward her, and she sighed in relief that he hadn't been hurt. She hadn't been able to tell before, but now it was clear that good old shifter healing had done him well. Crimson had dried over half of his face, but no cuts remained.

She walked toward him, tossing off the blanket

that had settled over her shoulders. Unable to help herself, she jogged, then ran and launched herself into his arms, desperate to feel his warmth and reassure herself that he was still here—still alive. He hesitated for the span of a breath, but then wrapped his powerful arms around her ribs and lifted her off the ground.

Burying his face against her hair, he inhaled deeply. "Tell me you're okay."

"Yes, yes, I'm fine. The paramedics cleared me. Just a little bit of a stiff neck and some tiny cuts and that's all. You shielded me from the worst of it and kept me from hitting the window, Boone. How did you react so fast?"

"I saw how scared your eyes were, and I don't know. I just reacted. I just needed you to be okay from whatever was coming."

"What kind of trouble are you in?" she breathed against his neck.

"The same kind we've always been in, Cora." His tone hardened. "But now it's worse because you are involved."

A new pair of headlights chased the shadows away for a moment, and she frowned at a solid black van, washed to shining. It stopped in front of Monroe's patrol car where he had locked their attacker in the back.

"Who's that?"

Boone settled her on her feet and turned. "That would be IESA's get-out-of-jail free card. Watch this."

A man in a suit that matched the attacker's exited the van and strode toward Monroe. He talked low and handed Monroe a sheet of paper, then crossed his arms over his chest and looked down his nose at the shorter police officer as he read it. Monroe shook his head slowly back and forth. When he looked up at the stranger, his eyes were filled with disbelief and fury. Clipped words cracked across the whipping breeze, but she didn't catch any of it.

"At least Monroe is fighting it," Cody said as he approached with the others.

"Yeah," Boone said. "Look there, the other deputies are arguing with him, too. Surprising. At least they are trying to get justice for us."

"Doesn't exist," Dade murmured from behind his alpha.

"But it will," Quinn said.

"Maybe," Cody muttered as the man handed

Monroe a cell phone, then sidled the officer and opened the back of the cop car. "But not tonight."

Cora guffawed. "Wait, they're releasing him? But he tried to kill us!"

Boone made a ticking sound behind his teeth and twitched his head. His odd-colored gaze flicked to her, reflecting oddly in the flashing lights, then panned to the gathered crowd on the sidewalk, about twenty strong now. "Not here, Cora. Come on."

Numbly, she followed the Kellers and their mates as she watched the police taking the handcuffs from the attacker's wrists. When he gave her a shark grin, full of dark promise that this wasn't over, fear chilled her from the middle out, turning her veins to ice.

Boone appeared beside her, blocking her view of the evil man as a soft snarl unfurled in his chest. Instant warmth flooded her as he draped his arm around her shoulders and pulled her against his side. His attention was on the man, but his fingers squeezed her upper arm in reassurance.

In Cody's jacked-up coal-colored truck, Cora leaned her head against the window. The tow truck drove by with Boone's demolished pickup.

"It's not fair," she gritted out as she dashed a tear

away with the back of her hand. "You love that truck, and that man is getting off free and clear. Not only does he get away with attempted murder, he doesn't even have to pay for damages he purposely inflicted on your ride. If you want it repaired, you'll have to pay for it out of pocket." She dragged her gaze to Boone who sat beside her in the back seat. "How is any of this right?"

"It's just a truck."

"Bullshit. You could drive whatever you want. You're single and have a good job. You drove that truck because it means something to you, and now it's all smashed up."

"Hm," Boone grunted with a slight furrow to his brow. "For a human, you see a lot."

"What does that mean?"

"It was our dad's truck," Cody said, turning the engine until it roared to life. "Boone got it in the will."

Rory turned and offered her a sad smile from the passenger seat. "Everything's going to be okay, Cora."

It didn't feel like anything would be okay ever again. She'd known the Kellers had lived a hard, secret life, and she'd felt for their plight, tried to make it easier on them even. But she hadn't realized it was like *this*. It was one thing to hear they had trouble with the IESA in their interview at town hall, but it was an entirely different matter to almost be killed at their hands, and just for associating with the Breck Crew.

And Boone...

God, he'd almost died tonight. If he'd been driving a small car or even a small truck, he wouldn't have walked away from this. That SUV had hit the front end right near him. Just the thought of him being hurt curdled her stomach.

Deny it out loud all she wanted to, but inside, Boone felt like hers.

She leaned over and kissed his shoulder, but his scent was off. It wasn't sweat, but something...bitter. "You smell different."

Boone pulled his tired gaze from the road passing under Cody's headlights to Cora. His nostrils flared as he inhaled near his shoulder. "It's Dade's shirt."

"No, it's not just that. I can tell the difference in your smell and the smell of the shirt. It's...anger?"

"Thata girl," Cody murmured, approval in his voice. "What else?"

She drew in another breath of air near his shoulder, snuggling closer. "Fur and...I don't know. Something deeper. Different."

"It's fear," Boone said in a somber, defeated voice. "Now you know. We're not invincible. Getting to us is as easy as trying to steal away the people we care about."

Cora's heart thumped hard against her sternum as it tethered to him a little more tightly. He cared. And not just as friends. On some base level, he'd connected with her as she'd connected with him. She wasn't the only one denying what was happening between them.

"You like me?" She regretted those needy words the second they left her lips. This wasn't the place, in the car with his brother and soon-to-be sister-in-law. After a wreck and an attack that almost cost them their lives. But then again, perhaps it was. Tonight proved that life was too damned short, and that it could be taken at any moment. And dammit, she was tired of games—tired of him pretending she meant less to him than she really did.

Boone didn't answer, only stared straight ahead, his body rigid against the side of her arm.

Slowly, she wrapped her arms around his middle and snuggled her cheek against his chest. "I like you back, Boone."

His body softened, and he released a shaky breath, then pulled her closer and kissed the top of her hair. He lingered there, his lips soft against her scalp. His scent was changing, drifting to the smell she'd grown to adore. The bitterness eased, and though she could still smell the difference in his shirt—a product of Dade's presence—Boone was coming back to her.

"I'm sorry about earlier," he murmured. "And about tonight, about the crash, and about everything. It wasn't ever my intention to complicate your life."

"Maybe my life needed complicating."

"Not like this," he said, shaking his head and resting his chin on her hair.

"It's done, Boone. Pushing me away isn't going to make me any safer now."

"Drawing you in even further isn't going to make you any safer either."

And that's where they disagreed. Boone hadn't cared about his own safety when he threw himself in front of the shattering glass to protect her. IESA and all the grit that came with being on their radar was scary. But the thought of cutting herself off from the protection Boone and the Breck Crew could provide felt even more dangerous. It was too late to go back to her normal life. Cody had been right when he'd said she was "in this now." She'd ghosted the sideline, defending a group of people she didn't know, but now her growing feelings for Boone had thrust her into the thick of it.

Whatever IESA's next move was, she wasn't any safer away from Boone.

EIGHT

The firehouse was all lit up when Cody stopped in front. Dade parked his truck behind, and they all piled out and made their way toward the open hangar.

Gage and two other men were undressing from their turn-out gear. The two human men working on shift both gave Boone rough hugs and said they were sorry about his dad's truck. It was clear in this station that bear shifter or human, it made no difference. They were a family, who had probably all saved each other's lives more than any of them would ever admit.

Boone introduced them as Jimmy and Barret, and they each shook her hand and said they were glad she was okay. One of them even offered to get her a blanket, which she happily agreed to. Though she still felt like she was walking on clouds with the shock of everything, Cora was still in the little black number she'd worn to the bar, and the chill had raised gooseflesh over every inch of her skin. Even the jacket Boone had given her wasn't enough to keep the frost in her veins at bay, and her teeth chattered on and on.

"It's a normal reaction to what happened. Traumatic events affect everyone differently, and tonight was a lot," Boone said low after she'd tried to duck and hide the blush in her cheeks. "You're a tough woman."

Startled, she jerked her attention to him, just to see if he was teasing. The fire in his eyes had cooled, and they were a stormy blue again, but there was no mockery in his gaze. Just pride.

"You did good handing me that knife when you did," he murmured against her ear as they followed his brothers past the fire engine and ambulance parked in the hangar.

"Flattery will get you everywhere with me, Boone." She'd stopped herself from calling him *Keller*.

She hated the way the IESA agent had called him that, and now she understood why Boone had balked against her using his surname. Never again.

A giant brindle-hound mix bounded up to her, tongue lolled out of his mouth in a doggy smile. She couldn't help the giggle that bubbled up her throat as he bounced around her like an oversize bunny rabbit.

"Tank, cut it out," Dade commanded, but there was a smile in his voice.

"Who's a good doggy?" she crooned, scratching under his chin. She'd always wanted a dog, but with her odd work hours at the news station, she hadn't the time to devote to one. As a result, she ended up playing with any dog she could get her scratching fingers on to make up for an empty home.

"Should've pegged you for a dog person," Dade said, hooking his hands on his hips.

"Why is that?" she asked, squatting down so she could snuggle Tank better. Damn, she needed this after the night she'd had.

"Because you like this animal," Dade joked, jerking his head toward Boone.

"You know," she said thoughtfully, "I could run it past the station to do a piece on firehouse dogs. It would do you guys good to be in a couple of shots playing with him. Good for public image." Cora scratched behind the dog's ears and laughed at his toothy mutt grin. "You wanna be famous, Tank?"

The dog perked his ears at his name and gave a little whine as he slurped his tongue back in his mouth.

"See?" Gage said from beside a row of lockers as he kicked out of a pair of heavy trousers. "This is why she'll be a good addition to the crew. She knows how to spin our image."

"She isn't a part of the crew," Boone gritted out.

Those words slashed against her heart, making her inhale sharply with the pain. Slowly, she stood and nodded. "I've had a long night, and I have no clue how long your meetings last. Would you all mind if we started so I can go home and get some rest?"

"Fuck," Boone muttered as she walked past him, following Cody toward a swinging door.

"Fuck is right," Rory muttered, pointing at Boone. "Fuck. Face." Her ruddy eyebrows were arched high, and Cora would've been intimidated by how fierce she looked if she could feel anything other than bone-deep confusion right now.

"Boone needs food," Cody said, guiding them through a hallway and into a large, open recreational room.

"Yeah, food should make him nicer," Cora grumbled sarcastically.

"No, but it'll help him heal."

Cora looked back at where Boone was trailing the crew, shaking his head at the ground. He linked his hands behind his head, and then flung them forward, muttering something she couldn't quite hear.

"He doesn't look hurt."

"Look closely at how he swings his arms. Cracked ribs and bad fractures would be my guess. Boone doesn't show pain. Never did. Food will get him feeling better. His attitude though? He's been like this for weeks, and I suspect it has something to do with you. Be patient with him. Boone's a hard one to crack."

"I can fuckin' hear you, Cody," Boone said, his voice deep and gravelly.

"Good," Cody snarled, turning so fast Cora almost ran into him. "Then play nice, because like it or not, she is right in the middle of this shit storm now.

Pushing her away like you're doing? If I did that to Rory, she'd filet me. Push Cora, and she'll do the same damned thing to you."

"I can fuckin' hear you, Cody," Cora repeated Boone's words in a soft voice, followed by a nervous laugh. She hated creating a riff between the Keller brothers. It didn't feel right to create fault lines in a family she respected so much.

Cody arched his blond brow and stared at her for a moment, then jammed his finger toward a bathroom sign. "Go clean up, Boone. I can't stand staring at you when you look like a murder victim."

Cora turned and gritted her teeth in an apologetic smile. She hadn't meant to get Boone in trouble with his brother...or no, his alpha. She didn't really know how all of this worked. The hierarchy was something she was going to have to ask Boone about later when he didn't have the face of a pissed-off berserker.

Boone dipped his chin to his chest, his hair falling forward across his face, and then lifted his gaze to Cora before he strode off toward the bathroom Cody had pointed to.

"I'll heat up the food," Gage said low, head canted

and neck exposed to Cody.

Electricity crackled through the air, making the room seem much smaller than it really was. Cora struggled to take a deep breath and took a step back from the alpha of the Breck Crew just to escape the heavy feeling that pressed against her chest.

"I'm going to go check on him," she whispered, unable to hold Cody's gaze. She spun and speed-walked after Boone, following him right into the men's restroom. He'd charged her private bathroom session earlier, so she gave exactly zero fucks if he disapproved now.

Except when she pushed open the swinging door, Boone didn't stop walking until he reached the other side of a row of urinals. He shoved another door open and left the bathroom. "Oooh, disobeying Cody's orders," she sang out low. She had the distinct feeling Cody could hold his own in a row with Boone, even after she'd seen him fight that IESA agent with deadly accuracy.

Boone didn't look back at her, though he must have known she was following. She was basically a drunken rhino when she walked, and her legs still felt wobbly on her high heels. He disappeared through a door but left it open.

Turning the corner, she halted, uncertain, then stepped slowly inside. It was a small room with a single bed and a closet. White walls and white tile ceilings, and the entire place looked sterile and bland.

Inside, Boone searched in a potted plant and then under the single table and desk chair. He narrowed his eyes and froze, head angled as if he was listening to something above her senses.

She closed the door with a soft click and leaned against it as Boone dragged the chair to the middle of the room and stood on it. He pushed a ceiling tile out of the way and yanked out something too small for her to identify. When Boone dropped it to the floor, she gasped at the small bug someone had planted in here. He stomped on it once, shattering it to dust, then slapped the back of the chair, blasting it against the wall.

She jumped at the explosive sound, but held her ground. Boone sank down onto the naked mattress and put his face in his hands. Back tensed, he screamed against his palms.

She hated seeing him like this because he was hurting.

She loved seeing him like this because he was allowing her to see him hurt.

"I didn't mean to get you in trouble."

"I fucking deserved it." His voice came out hoarse, tugging at her heart. With a sigh, he admitted, "I don't know what to do."

"About me?"

"About anything. That was my dad's truck. The only thing I have left of him. He died and left us reeling, but when he was here, me and him fixed that stupid thing up together. I should be broken up about it, but all I can think about, over and over, was the fear in your eyes right before we were hit."

"You're scared to get attached to me because it would hurt to lose me."

Boone cast her an angry glance over his shoulder, but his irritation wasn't with her. She could tell. It was with himself.

"You don't want to like me."

"It's not that I don't want to, Cora. It feels so fucking good to be around you. It's that I'm scared of what will happen. Two tours and a dangerous job, and I've never been afraid. Not like this."

"Cody was right, though. Pushing me away isn't

going to fix any of this. It'll only hurt me."

"You don't even know me. You don't know the man I am or the shit I've been through." His voice dipped low. "The shit I've *done*."

"Then explain it all to me."

"So you can run? So you can look scared and see me like everyone else—a monster?" He was shaking now, the acrid scent of his anger and fear filling the room until it was hard to breathe.

She fought her instinct to give him space and kicked off her heels, then settled them neatly against the wall. With a deep, steadying breath, she stepped around the bed and straddled his lap. Heart in her throat, she slid her arms out of the sleeves of his oversize jacket, then wrapped it around them like a blanket. Resting her cheek carefully against his taut chest, she whispered, "Boone Leland Keller, I'm not going anywhere. Pushing me away won't work."

His whole body trembled under her as he slid his hands under the jacket and around her waist. Dragging her closer, he searched her eyes, as if questioning whether she knew what she was doing.

"I'm scared, too," she murmured, cupping his cheeks. "It's okay. Tonight was terrifying and eye-opening, but we're okay. Now, let me see."

A muscle twitched under his eye, and she thought he would deny her. Instead, he eased back just far enough to pull Dade's sweater over his head.

She gasped as she saw the smooth skin over his ribcage, all red and blue, bruised badly from the indentation between his six pack to his side. "Boone," she whispered, running her finger softly around the outside of the dark coloring.

"This proves that dick was IESA. This is a move Krueger taught all his recruits. I should've protected that side better, but I was fighting distracted. I kept wanting to draw him closer to you, just so I could make sure there wasn't a second agent waiting in the wings."

Cora shrugged out of his jacket and set it on the bare mattress next to him. His perfect little nipples drew up in the cold vent air, and she smiled as she leaned down and pulled one into her mouth.

"Damn, woman," he groaned, rocking his hips against her.

The little black dress she was wearing had slipped up her thighs when she'd straddled him, and now her panties and his jeans were the only barrier between them.

Boone leaned back on his locked arms and stretched back, giving her more room to work as she moved to his other nipple and drew it into her mouth. Tiny sucks followed by a nibble, and he rolled against her again.

Drawing up suddenly, he captured her lips with his and drove his tongue into her mouth. A helpless sound wrenched from her chest as she rocked against him.

Angling his head, he deepened the kiss and cupped her sex with his hand. She should've been embarrassed by how wet her panties already were, but she couldn't conjure enough energy for shame. She'd almost died tonight. No time was promised to anyone, and she wanted Boone to settle the fear that had constricted her chest since the wreck.

Damn, Boone was big. Even like this, she could tell his erection was long and thick. Intimidatingly so, but she still wanted him worse than anything right now.

"Touch me," she demanded, gripping his hair in the back.

He didn't even wince as she brushed his ribs. His

pupils were so dilated, his eyes were almost black. Without hesitation, he pulled her panties to the side and brushed a sensitive spot that made her gasp and arch her back.

"You said you never came with a man before," Boone said in a soft voice.

"I haven't."

"Truth," he said. "I can hear it."

"You gonna make me come, Boone? You gonna make me fuck your hand like you said earlier?"

"Mmm," he rumbled, plucking her lips with his, tasting her. "I like your filthy mouth."

"Good. Make me come, and I'll suck your dick. I'll make you feel better."

"Trouble," he accused through a wicked grin.

"Better believe it."

He slid his long finger inside of her, thumbing her clit when he was buried up to his knuckle.

"Oh, my gosh," she panted out, wrapping her arms around his neck so she could ride him better. How the man knew exactly where to touch her was beyond her comprehension. She barely knew her body that well.

With desperate fingers, she reached between

them and unbuttoned his jeans. "Want to touch you," she murmured as she lifted off him and pulled his briefs down, unsheathing his dick. His beautiful, swollen to redness, tipped-with-creamy-moisture dick.

She exhaled a shuddering sigh as she settled on top of it. She rocked, forcing Boone's hand to rub himself. His thighs tensed under her and that soft, feral noise rattled his throat again.

"Changed my mind," she whispered, grazing her teeth against his neck. "I don't want to fuck your hand."

She'd lost her mind completely. Usually, she was the controlled one, the one who kept a clear head in every situation, but right now, all she could think about was touching Boone's thick shaft with her wet sex. She pushed his hand until his finger came out of her, then grinned like a goddess when he drew it in his mouth and sucked her taste off it.

"It's your show now, Trouble."

She just wanted to fool around a bit, tease them both a little. Settling onto him, she rolled her eyes back as her body pulsed at just touching his smooth skin there. Back and forth she moved, sliding over his shaft until he was slick with her wetness. He was a good bear at first, still for her. By the fourth stroke, however, he reached forward under the hem of her pushed-up dress. A tiny rip sounded, and then another, and her panties were in a little shredded pile on the floor.

"Clever bear," she said against his mouth.

She drew his bottom lip against her teeth. When she did, he bucked against her, as if he couldn't help himself. "You like me bitey? Of course, you do. You liked when I slapped your arm earlier in the bar, didn't you?" She leaned forward and gently nibbled his ear.

His hands gripped her waist and he jerked against her again, thighs tense as his breath came in shaky pants.

"Again," he said.

She pressed her teeth against his neck, and he groaned and rocked his hips harder.

Pressure was filling her, expanding in her until she was ready to explode with it. The slick, rhythmic sound of them rubbing against each other's sexes filled the room in the most erotic noise she'd ever heard.

"Boone," she said on a breath. "I'm going to come."

"Fffuck," he growled out, gripping her waist and slamming her against him.

Desperation filled her to be closer to him—to be part of him. She'd never wanted to be connected to a man so badly. "I'm on the pill," she huffed out.

Boone was straining now and his dick was so swollen between her lips. His hips jerked like he'd lost control. She fucking loved this.

"You know what you're asking?" he asked through clenched teeth. His neck muscles strained as he bucked against her again.

"I want to come with you inside of me," she said against his ear.

The growling in his chest grew louder as he reached between their legs and pushed the head of his shaft upward. She took him, sliding down until she stretched around all of him.

"Bite me, bite me, bite me," he chanted breathily.

She slid up and down him as a cry of ecstasy built in her throat. To silence it, she clamped her teeth on his neck.

"Harder," he demanded, pushing in and out of

her.

She sank her teeth into his skin as she came. Boone gripped her hair and shoved her even closer as he rammed into her again and froze.

His breath came in gasps as his body jerked with every stream of warmth he shot into her. Cora's body pulsed around him, her orgasm crashing through her as she released his torn neck and rested her forehead against his shoulder. The pleasure was so intense between her legs she whispered his name over and over.

All the fear from before leached from her with every aftershock.

Here, in his arms, she was safe and coveted.

Here, no one could get to her.

Here, tangled up with Boone, and despite everything that had happened tonight, she was happy.

NINE

Cora stretched her arms above her head and stared in confusion at the unfamiliar ceiling fan above her. Exposed wooden beams contrasted against the cream color of the room. She lifted the sheets with a frown and stared down at the dress she'd worn last night, still clinging to her body, minus her panties. Those, Boone had unapologetically shoved into his jeans pocket before they went out to meet the rest of the Kellers for the Breck Crew meeting.

Mortification heated her cheeks as she remembered how awkward she'd felt trying to keep a straight face after what she and Boone had done in his room at the station, especially with him flashing those sexy smiles when everyone's attention was diverted.

What should've been an intensely serious meeting about their next move to stay safe from the new IESA threat had ended up not quite as scary as she'd imagined.

This must be Boone's room. She recognized it from that stupid video those jerks had posted. Plus, the pillow smelled good, like him when he was content.

She rolled over to search with her legs for cool pockets under the sheets, but froze at the long gashes in the comforter and mattress. The sheets were ripped, and one of the pillows was bleeding stuffing. What the hell?

She sat ramrod straight, clutching her chest as she dragged her horrified gaze over the long claw marks on the wall next to the bed.

A rhythmic *thwack thwack* echoed through the house, and Cora stood on shaky legs. Stepping gingerly over a broken end table and shattered alarm clock, she approached an opened window. Why did he need to sleep with an open window when it was so cold out?

Outside, Boone's smooth, bare shoulder muscles

moved with lithe grace as he slammed an ax down on a piece of firewood. He shoved the split pieces off into a pile and put another one on the chopping block in a smooth motion as if he'd repeated this action a million times before. The unwavering arc of the blade slamming down on this piece of wood said that perhaps he had.

He wore jeans that had gone threadbare in places and work boots, but nothing else to ward away the crisp morning air.

She looked around the destroyed room again and shook her head in disbelief. He must have had a dream that made him shift again, like in the video, and somehow, she'd slept right through it. Twisting, she stared at the long claw marks down the bed. They couldn't have been more than three inches from where she'd been sleeping.

Too close.

Okay, Boone was obviously working through some demons if the sound of relentless wood chopping was anything to go by. Avoiding another peek at the shredded bed, she made her way carefully to the bathroom. She must've fallen asleep on the way over here, and Boone obviously had carried her inside and tucked her in for the night, so she hadn't seen the outside, but she'd imagined he lived in a rustic cabin in the woods. This bathroom was all custom tiling and fancy framed mirrors and brushed nickel finishes, though. And it was also spotless, which didn't fit the bachelor stereotype, which reminded her of how very little she still knew of Boone.

She'd checked out of the condo in the middle of the night at Boone's request. He'd said he wanted her somewhere safe where he could protect her, and she understood. She wanted to protect him from the IESA, too, even though he'd already survived more than she would likely ever know about.

He'd helped her pack, and she hadn't even had the energy to be embarrassed when he saw how destroyed her bathroom was. She wasn't as tidy as Boone seemed to be and worked better with her morning beauty routine if she could reach everything easily and not be digging products out of drawers.

On his shining marble countertop, he'd placed her bag of toiletries and lined up her straightening iron, curling iron, and blow dryer in a neat row. Maybe bear shifters needed organization. With this thought in mind, she put her toothbrush and toothpaste back after she was done with them and tucked away her hair styling tools under the sink. A-plus for Cora, but her reflection in the mirror was one rude heifer. "Ow, ow, ow," she whispered as she pulled a butterfly bandage from the cuts on her cheek.

She tossed the shower a thoughtful glance as the measured chopping sounded on.

With a sigh, she slipped into a pair of flip flops and made her way through the living room with its matching high ceiling and exposed beams and out the front door.

"Oh," she murmured, turning to look at the front of the house. It wasn't a cabin at all, but a Victorian style home with evergreen-colored siding and cream trim. Fragrant landscaping extended around the front corners, and the small overhang over the front door was propped up with natural cedar posts. The house looked like it belonged in one of those fine furniture magazines.

She swung her gaze to Boone, who had to have known she was there but kept on chopping firewood, anyway. His tattoos connected from his wrist to his shoulder, and his hair was pulled away from his face with a backward hat. His muscles rippled with every swing, and his intense eyes were gold, or perhaps an odd shade of green, in the bright morning light. He did not strike her as the type of man who enjoyed home decoration, but clearly, he was.

Damn, it was sexy when a man could surprise her like that.

Cora made her way around the curving landscaping to sit on a bench near where he worked. It was cold, and she should've worn a jacket, so she tucked her legs under her to conserve her body heat.

"Do you want to take a shower with me?" she asked after a few minutes of watching him.

"Woman, I'm not going to be a gentle lay right now," he growled out.

"I wouldn't mind a rough fuck from you, Boone, but that's not what I asked. I'm asking for intimacy."

He jerked the ax to a halt mid-swing and settled it beside him, then leaned on it and canted his head as he searched her face. "What's the difference?"

She snorted. Typical alpha male. "The difference is I want to touch you. I want you to hold me after everything that happened and convince my body that everything is going to be okay. Have you ever slept with a woman before?"

Boone rolled his neck and picked up another log to chop. "Cora, you aren't my first."

"I didn't say fuck. I said slept with."

Boone chucked the wood he was about to cut across the clearing with a feral sound in his throat. "No, I haven't. And there's a reason for that. I thought it would be different with you, but I still had the nightmares and I still shifted in my sleep. And this time, I almost hurt you before I had my mind. Next time, it could be worse. That can't happen again. I'm sleeping on the couch from here on."

Silence stretched on between them as he scanned his woods, avoiding her gaze. At last, when it was clear he was doing a bang-up job of engaging in a mental war she didn't have access to, she cleared her throat. "I was a goth kid in high school, if you can believe it. Dyed black hair with bright purple streaks, fishnets peeking through the holes in my jeans, black lipstick, white foundation, the works."

Boone sighed, the knots in his shoulders relaxing. He turned and sat on the bench beside her. "Why?"

"I was emotional about everything, and it had to do with how angry I was with the world. No, it wasn't the world I was pissed at. It was my mom. My dad was never in the picture, and my mom liked to party. My Grandma Ruth raised me. And you know, I had a really awesome childhood because she made it as normal as possible, but there was this hole in me. There was this gnawing ache that told me over and over that I wasn't enough to make my mom want to get her life back on track. And I swear, as soon as I would accept she was just not meant to be a mother, she would come back around for a week, clear-eyed, talking about how she'd changed and was trying to be better so she could take me home. Except I never knew what home she was talking about. The only place I'd ever known was a two-bedroom apartment in Denver I shared with my Grandma Ruth and two goldfish. But that didn't matter because I'd still get my hopes up that my mom was getting her shit together for me. I went to a few community college classes, and one of them was an elective. I thought it would be an easy A to keep my Grandma Ruth off my back, but it changed my life."

"What class was it?"

"Journalism. Everything seemed so clear after that semester. I let my hair go back to my natural blond and softened my make-up. I worked at this diner and saved up until I could afford—and you better not laugh because you've probably already noticed—but I got a boob job because I was told no one was going to hire me for television with a 32-A chest."

"Ah," he said nodding. "I wondered. I love your big tits, Cora, but you would've been just as beautiful with your 32-As. You know that, right?"

"I do now, but I had a lot of growing to do to get here."

"Okay, so why are you telling me all this?"

"Because now it's your turn. What are the nightmares about?"

He let off a growl and took his hat off, then replaced it, as if it was a nervous habit. Leaning his elbows on his knees, he stared out at the tree line. "They're about losing everyone. IESA chasing us, gunfire, watching my family die one by one, even the cubs. And the end is always the same. You die in my arms."

"Me?"

"Yeah. I can never save you. I can't save anyone."

"But…" She tried to wrap her head around what he was saying. "That video of your nightmare was taken before you met me."

"Yeah, I must've seen you on the news or something. Come on. I'll take a shower with you, and I probably won't even turn into a bear."

"Boone," she called, following him into the house. "Why would you have nightmares about me dying if you didn't even know me?"

"How the hell should I know? I'm not some dream expert. I don't want to talk about it anymore, Cora. Please. It doesn't make me feel any better."

"Okay," she said uncertainly.

Boone hit the hot tap in the shower and shed his jeans. Now, shyness crept over Cora in light of his admission. He'd thought about her before he'd met her, enough to dream about her. Something unsettling lingered in her mind—an idea that was just out of reach.

"Let me," he murmured, unzipping her dress in back. His touch was soft as he pushed the fabric off her shoulders.

His warm hands gripped her tense neck and

massaged it just right, not too hard, not too soft. "How are you feeling today?"

She groaned in ecstasy and rolled her head back against his chest. "Neck is stiff, but if you keep that up, I'll be back to one hundred percent in no time."

"What time do you have to be at work?"

"Seven tonight. No fun assignments today unless one of my contacts gives me a tip, just the nine o'clock news. I used to have a police scanner I would listen to for leads, which is how I found out about that veterinary clinic fire where you and your brothers came out to the public. I left it at the house I shared with Eddie, though. I need to go back and get all of my belongings at some point. I just haven't been ready to face him yet."

Boone massaged little circles down the muscles that bracketed her spine.

"I need to pick up some dry-cleaning before work so I have something to wear tonight, though. The station isn't big enough for a wardrobe department."

"Ah, I see," he said, guiding her toward the steaming shower.

When they settled under the hot jets of water

and leaned against the wall facing each other, Boone brushed her cheek with his knuckle and said, "My father was a bit of a lying asshole, too, if it makes you feel any better."

Cora grabbed his hand to keep his touch and murmured, "That doesn't make me feel better. I don't like you being hurt."

"You're protective as a momma bear, you know that?"

"Damn straight. You're mine—" Cora gasped and wished she could swallow the words back down. She hadn't meant to utter those words out loud. Now, Boone would push and run like he always did.

His eyes went wide and serious, and his chest heaved as water trickled down the ends of his hair that draped in front of his face. "Say that again."

In a voice as meek as a mouse, she said, "You're mine."

"Come here," he demanded low.

He hugged her tight and maneuvered her around until her back was under the warm jets of water. His stony erection pressed against her belly, but he didn't act on it. He only pressed his lips against her wet hair and rocked them back and forth in a music-less slow dance.

"You aren't going to push me away this time?"

"What's the point?" he murmured in that sexy, gravelly voice. "You're in danger either way, and I'm sick of torturing us."

"What happened with your father?"

"Titus Keller was an upstanding citizen and a great father. He was a firefighter, and the reason I wanted to be one, too. He was perfect, until he wasn't. IESA hit his kill switch while he was fighting a fire."

"Kill switch?"

Boone eased her back and lifted his chin, exposing a thin pink scar on his neck. "We had trackers in us that IESA could detonate when we lost our usefulness. It's where Dade got that chemical burn on his neck, and it's why Cody's hand looks melted. Cody got mine out first but wasn't fast enough with Dade's, and Krueger, our handler at the time, pushed the kill switch when Cody had Dade's tracker halfway out. I still feel like shit that Cody took mine out first. Dade is my younger brother. It should've been me who got burned, not him."

Horror filled her chest at his words. "Wait, why would Krueger want to kill you?"

"Because we weren't playing by his rules."

"Which were?"

"Do everything he says, no matter what. He was blackmailing us with exposure to the human public if we didn't do these black ops missions for him. I killed... Fuck, you should know what you're in this with. I killed people."

"You were at war. I know you did two tours."

"Yeah, there, but here, too. Krueger told us we were keeping terrorist threats under control, but it turned out he was just having us kill other shifters who weren't useful to him anymore. When we found out, we balked, and he tried to end us. He even had...well, you heard it in the meeting at town hall. He had trackers in Gage's cubs, too, but we didn't have any idea they were kill switches. He kidnapped Rory and called us with her location. We knew we were walking into a trap, but if that was our last stand, we were going to do it together, me and Dade and Cody. We left Gage with Ma and the cubs in case we couldn't get out of there, and he had strict instructions to take the crew underground if things went south. We barely made it out of there, and only because my half-brother, Bruiser, showed up."

"You have a half-brother? Was he the dark-headed man at the back of the room in town hall? He had strange colored eyes, like yours."

"Yeah. Bruiser was part of Dad's hidden family. I told you my dad was a lying asshole? He had this entire secret life while I was growing up. He'd convinced everyone he'd bonded to Ma, but he hadn't. If he was bonded to her like he said he was, he wouldn't have been able to go behind her back and breed someone else. His mistress died having Bruiser, but Dad hired a nanny for him and raised him not thirty miles from here. Bruiser came to us right after Dad died, and it broke Ma. Just shredded her, and I hated my dad for what he'd done to her." Boone shook his head as he clenched his teeth so hard his jaw muscles twitched. "He'd worked on that damned truck with me every chance he got, and never once did he mention any of the awful ways he was betraying our family, betraying Bruiser."

"Oh, Boone, I'm so sorry." Her mom had been a wreck, but at least Cora had always known where she stood with her. Boone had grown up thinking his father was this perfect hero, but he had betrayed them all along, for years.

"Nah, don't worry about it. It's done now. Maybe that stupid truck was supposed to be demolished. It was my way of clinging to the good memories I had of my dad." He poured shampoo into his hands and massaged her scalp.

She smiled despite the heaviness of their conversation because this dominant apex predator and alpha sexpot man was shampooing her hair with a gentleness that surprised her.

"What?" he asked through a questioning smile.

"You're really good at this."

"Well, I have longer hair so I know how to shampoo, Cora. That's not exactly trophy worthy."

"Not just shampooing my hair. I mean, you're good at balancing your life. Last night, you were in this intense hand-to-hand combat with a highly trained operative, and now, those same hands that pummeled him are gently washing my hair. Deep down, you are a softy, Boone Leland Keller."

A soft growl rumbled from him as he tilted her head back and began to rinse her under the showerhead. "Only with you. And if you tell anyone, I swear I'll deny it."

"Your secret is safe with me. Boone?" She

gripped his wrists and steadied him stroking her hair.

"Yeah?"

"All of your secrets are safe with me."

TEN

"Here," Boone said, offering her another slice of strawberry.

Cora opened her mouth from her seated position on his kitchen countertop. The sweetness burst against her tongue.

He chuckled so she asked, "What's so funny?"

"You kick your legs like a kid at sleepaway camp when you taste good food."

"Do not."

"Do so, and what is that you're fiddling with?"

"It looks kind of strange, but it's a video camera," she said sarcastically. "Maybe you've seen one on the history channel? Not everything is done on phones, you know. There are these complicated contraptions called cameras whose sole purpose is to take photographs and video."

"All right, smartass, what are you going to be using that ancient gadget for?"

"Cody is organizing the interviews for tomorrow, and I'm kind of nervous. I haven't run a camera since college."

"What about hiring the cameraman who shoots for your assignments?" Boone asked as he scooped up the fruit salad he'd made into a plastic storage container.

"Carl?" The camera was fully charged, so she pulled the cord from it and opened the viewing screen. "Because I don't trust him. Not with you and your family. He's on the fence if he is for or against you having to register as shifters with the government, and I know for a fact he voted against having you reinstated in the fire department."

Cody rinsed his hands and dried them, then threw the dish towel over his shoulder and leaned against the counter. "And how do you know that?"

"Because he wasn't exactly quiet about it in the break room at work. The station is divided on how they feel about you guys. I don't want someone assisting me on an interview who doesn't have a clear agenda. Sorry, chum. It'll just be me this time around."

"Hmm." Eyes narrowed, he pulled the camera from her grasp and hit record, then turned it on her. "Cora Wright, on a scale of one to ten, how terrifying is it landing the first exclusive interview with a secretive crew of bear shifters?"

She grinned and played along. "I'd say about an eleven. Bear shifters can Change whenever they want to, and what if they get a hankering for human à la mode? I'd be toast."

Boone snorted and shook his head. "We bears would probably rather eat the toast." He leaned forward and kissed her smiling lips, settling his hips between her thighs. "And strawberries, and you taste like those right now. Maybe you're in danger after all." A soft growl rattled his throat as he leaned in and kissed her again, a sweet smack on her lips.

"Are you growling at me? Well, grrr to you." Her growl was borderline pathetic, but Boone looked appropriately scared and clutched his chest, eyes wide, though he couldn't quite seem to lose the grin.

"And though she be but little, she is fierce,"

Boone murmured, looking at the camera he held in front of them.

Butterflies flapped around her stomach. "Wait, did you just recite Shakespeare?"

"Does that surprise you?"

"Tatted up bad boy bear shifter reciting lines from A Midsummer Night's Dream? I couldn't be more surprised." She canted her head and let the smile fall away from her face. "Or happy. How am I supposed to keep my heart if you say things like that to me?"

"You aren't," he murmured, matching her serious tone. "You're supposed to give it to me."

"Aw," she said, feeling giddy down to her toes.

Boone set the camera down and pulled her off the counter. Her feet dangled in the air as he hugged her tight and inhaled deeply against her hair.

"You should bring your camera. You can get comfortable with it on our hike, then you won't have to be nervous using it tomorrow."

"We're going on a hike?"

"Yeah, I want to show you something."

"What is it?"

Boone eased back and smiled as he searched her

eyes. "I'm going to show you *me*."

She nearly squealed, "Really?"

"Really, really."

"Can I pet you?"

"Cora," Boone warned.

"I won't tell your brothers."

Boone set her on her feet and shook his head as if she was being unreasonable. A grin still ghosted his lips though, so she didn't feel too bad about the request.

"Please, I've seen your bear twice now, and you look soft."

"Oh, geez. Fine. Fine, just stop calling me soft."

Cora ran her feet in place, and then stood up on tiptoes, kissing him on the underside of his smooth shaven chin. "You are soft for me."

"Cora—"

"I know, I know! Don't tell your brothers." She giggled and bounded off to grab her hiking boots.

Boone was opening up to her, little by little, and something about that made her insides feel like they were glowing. She'd been afraid he would shut her out and hurt her like Eddie had, but Boone wasn't anything like Eddie. He was a good man, a protective one, who tried when she needed more.

And despite the gravity of what had happened yesterday, he was letting her see his playful side. The one she'd seen him have with his brothers after the town meeting. The happy mood that had enamored her and made her heart thump oddly in her chest when she'd seen him in the hallway clapping Cody on the back, saying something too low for her to hear but that made his entire crew laugh. And his smile... She hadn't given too much thought to Boone at the town hall meeting back then, but now, pieces were coming back to her. Important moments that she was glad she remembered now. The color of his bear when he'd Changed near the vet clinic with his brothers for the first time, when she'd hidden behind the fire engine in fear. The way he hovered protectively around the cubs in the Breck Crew when they walked into town hall, heads held high and proud despite the mixed emotions from the crowds. They'd locked eyes in the meeting, she and Boone, for just a moment before she glanced away, unable to hold his gaze.

They had connected somehow, even back then. There was something that had hovered in the air between them, drawing her to him. Some magnetic force that said their story together had only just begun, but she'd been helpless to see it back then.

Now, everything seemed so clear.

Eddie wasn't meant to be hers. He hadn't known what to do with a strong woman and had acted out with mistresses, trying to prove his dominance in the relationship. It had been a challenge for him to accept his girlfriend was as successful as him. Eddie wrote for the town newspaper and was accomplished at his job, but she was recognizable when they went out together because of her time in front of the camera. Her success as a reporter was a constant battle between her and Eddie, but Boone was the type of man who was secure with himself. He was strong and required a strong woman to weather the things he and his crew had to endure.

With Boone, her strength was an asset, not a hindrance.

And now, it was becoming obvious she'd been meant to have that draining relationship with Eddie so that she could fully appreciate Boone's good qualities.

When she re-emerged in her hiking boots and

heavy jacket, Boone was zipping up a backpack full of their brunch. His greeting smile just about buckled her knees. "You look gorgeous, Trouble."

She dragged her appreciative gaze up his powerful jean-clad legs to the sky blue sweater that clung to his fit physique. The color of his shirt made his eyes look even brighter under his baseball cap. "You're not so bad yourself, you hunky bear."

A deep chuckle sounded from Boone's chest as he shouldered the backpack. "You know," he said, leading her out the front door, "you're a lot different than I imagined from seeing you on the news."

"Everybody says that." She snatched the camera from the counter and flipped the screen closed. "The personality you see on television is my professional one. What people don't realize is that it's just a job, and when we go home at night, we have our own lives and opinions and ups and downs. I try to maintain my public image when I'm out and about in town, but I think it's a little harder to do in a smaller place. If I'd landed a job in Denver, the city would be big enough that I might not get recognized as much. Here, sometimes I feel like I always have to be on. You know what I mean?" The lawn was dry from the autumn season, but still springy under her shoes. Boone's yard was probably impeccable in the spring and summer months.

"I know exactly what you mean." Boone waited, halting his strides long enough for her to catch up. "If I screw up for even a second, it could mean awful things for my family. The entire Breck Crew is feeling the pressure right now. But then again, we've always had to hide, so I'm kind of used to the public image gig."

"Yeah, I didn't think about that. It's probably a lot harder for you than me. Messing up for me would just cost me my job. But for you, it could mean stricter rules for you, your cubs being banned from public schools, or shifter registration."

"It feels like people are just waiting for us to mess up. Like last night. That could've gone really bad if you hadn't taken that video and showed it to Monroe when he was taking your statement. Your quick thinking probably kept me from a night in jail while they corroborated everyone's story."

She shivered when she thought about Boone shifting inside of a tiny jail cell at the local police station. At least when he'd had an uncontrolled

Change here, he had been able to get out of his house and find woods immediately.

"You know, humans aren't all bad. I have tons of footage of people protesting your treatment, who want equal rights for you. It's not just me and the Blue Haired Ladies advocating for you. There is an entire country-wide movement. It's like online. People are mostly wonderful and supportive when they talk about me on the station's webpages, but it's just that one harsh remark that hurts so much and negates all of the positive ones. I don't know why it's like that. What right does one negative comment have to outweigh all of the positive?"

Boone shot her a sideways glance, then stared ahead quietly as they made their way around a snarl of brambles across the trail.

"I like the way you see things," he said at last. "You see the good in people. The honest parts."

"There's lots of good to see, Boone. The meanest people are usually the loudest. Get past them and you'll see the chain of support that is growing every day."

"I know you're right," he murmured, offering his hand as she climbed up onto a mossy tree stump.

Up here, she was as tall as Boone, so she threw her arms around his neck and tossed her hair out of her face. "Say it again."

Boone huffed a laugh, and the corners of his eyes crinkled with his smile. "You're right. I can tell because of the online forums we've been answering questions in. There was a lot of hatred there at first. It was hard continuing without telling them all to shut the fuck up. But then the coolest thing started happening. Other people started defending us, and after a while, we had to only respond to those angry questions once, then the others in the forum would take over and cut off inappropriate commenters. Rory said the same thing, that she could see it getting better. She's the one online the most, trying to dispel rumors."

"It'll get better and better, Boone. You'll see."

His eyes softened and he leaned forward, then bit her neck gently. "I think the government has lost control of the IESA."

Cora pulled his baseball hat off and replaced it backward so she could see his face better. "What do you mean?"

"I mean, last night was sloppy. IESA going after

me in town with a shitty-placed wreck, and trying to take you, a well-known public figure down, too? That's amateur shit. Krueger kidnapping Rory was sloppy before that. I think they are pulling desperate measures to remain a relevant agency."

"Good. I hope the government finds out what they've been doing and burns the IESA to the ground."

"And how are they going to find out? We have to walk such a fine line between defending ourselves against IESA and admitting what we've done for them. The public won't accept us if they knew what we were forced to do for Krueger."

"You didn't have a choice."

Boone shook his head sadly. "There is always a choice, Cora."

Cora bit her bottom lip and nuzzled his cheek with hers. Pulling her chin back, she pressed her lips onto his. No more talk of the past and things he couldn't control. She wanted right now with him, the part where they'd both survived IESA and lived for this moment.

Boone cupped her head as she tasted him, brushed her tongue against his. That soft, approving rumble rattled his throat and revved her up. Heat pooled between her legs when he dragged her waist closer, pressed her against his erection. She imagined him inside of her again and a soft moan left her lips.

Cora shoved the straps of the backpack off his shoulders. His hat hit the ground, and she scrambled to lift the hem of his shirt over his head. The bruises on his ribs were almost healed, but she kissed him there, anyway.

"Why'd you do that?" he murmured, looking at her with the most curious expression.

"So it'll feel better. Does it?"

He frowned in disbelief down at his torso and nodded. "Yeah."

She grinned triumphantly and unzipped her jacket. Boone's hands went to her chest immediately as she shrugged out of it. He cupped her, then blew warm air onto her sweater, right over one of her nipples. It drew up taut at the sensation. Arching back, she exhaled languidly, closing her eyes against the sunlight filtering through the canopy above.

Boone pulled her shirt over her head and popped her tits out of her bra, then pushed them together and sucked on one of her nipples. Holy hell balls, she loved him like this. In control, focused, adoring her body and casting away all of her insecurities. This wasn't a lights-off-five-minute-fuck like it had been with Eddie. This was heart-pounding, pussy-pulsing, desperate-for-touch love-making with a man who made her feel like she was everything.

The slow rip of her zipper was the sexiest thing she'd ever heard, but he only pulled her pants down just enough to slip his hand in and cup her sex.

"Damn, woman, I love how you soak your panties for me."

She gasped sharply as he slid his long finger inside of her and brushed her clit with his palm. He stroked again, and she rolled her hips, setting the pace as she clutched onto his shoulders.

"Boone," she panted on a breath.

"Fuck, yes, more of that."

"Harder."

He bit her bottom lip hard enough to burn as he pressed his finger in deeper and faster.

"I'm gonna—"

"Come for me, baby," Boone murmured against her ear.

Her body exploded around him, pulsing with

blinding pleasure as she bowed against him and cried out. She raked her nails across his back as he pressed into her again and again, drawing out her aftershocks.

"That's two times now, Trouble. Two orgasms from a man."

Cora rubbed her cheek against his as he stroked her slowly, pulling every last pleasurable throbbing sensation from her satiated body. "You keeping score, Boone?"

"Hell yeah, I am. We're just getting started, you and me."

"Really?" Hope bloomed in her chest as the first tingle of pressure began to build in her middle again.

"You ever had someone fuck you like a werebear?" Boone laughed as he ducked her swat.

"Boone Leland Keller, you would bring up Nasty Eddie right now, wouldn't you? I think my vagina is drying up."

"It's not," Boone said, nibbling her lip as he slid his finger inside of her again with a slick sound.

"Well, keep talking about my ex, and it'll shrivel up and blow away. Just dust in the wind. And besides, I can't imagine that being fun for the girl. Eddie's side-chick sounded like she was faking it."

Boone's lips dipped to her neck, and he trailed down to her collar bone with biting, sucking kisses. When she looked down, he had himself in hand, stroking. A drop of moisture sat at the tip, and she lowered herself and sat on the mossy trunk. His finger slid from her, but that was okay. She wanted to make him feel good now. She kissed the salty drop from his erection and teased the swollen head of his cock with her tongue.

Boone groaned and jerked his hips forward.

"So sensitive," she whispered. She gripped him at the base and applied pressure.

Boone inhaled sharply as she slid him into her mouth. His hips and legs flexed as if he couldn't help himself.

Cora pulled his hands behind her head and eased off him. "Tell me what you like, but be gentle about it, yeah?"

Boone's nostrils flared as he nodded his head sharply. She smiled at the fact his eyes had gone that gold-green color and he looked completely feral right now. She'd done that to him, pushed him to the edge of his control.

His finger entwined with her hair, and he pushed her slowly over him. "Touch yourself," he rasped out.

With a wicked little smile for him, she spread her knees wider and slid her hand under the elastic of her panties, then rocked her hips as she pressed her finger inside of herself.

Boone's breath came in short pants now, and when she looked up, his pupils had dilated to pinpoints, his focus between her legs.

His grip tightened in her hair as she set a faster pace on him, to match what felt good as she took care of herself.

"Fuck, Cora," he growled out as his hips jerked faster.

His body tensed, matching how her insides felt. Arms tight, breath rushed, his eyes intent on where she was pushing into herself.

Pressure, God, the pressure between her legs.

"Stop, or I'm going to come in your mouth," Boone gritted out.

Pulling her mouth off him, she gasped out his name, then leaned back on a locked arm and plunged her finger into herself again.

"Not without me, Trouble," he said, pulling her

up. Boone spun her and yanked her jeans down. Bending her forward, he gripped her hips with one hand, and used the other to guide his dick into her from behind. She was ready for it, wet and stretched out, so desperate to feel him inside of her that the tightness she should've felt wasn't there.

Locking her arms against the stump, she arched back to give him a better angle, and he pushed into her again. Boone trailed gentle bites up her spine, then slammed into her again. She gasped, rocked by how good he felt like this.

"Harder," she begged.

Boone growled and thrust into her with more force. Desperate to feel him, she reached back and cupped her sex where he was sliding in and out of her. Her swollen clit was so sensitive, all it took was a touch from her fingertip and her nerve endings went crazy.

"Oh!" she cried, arching, arching, inviting him to drive into her as hard as he liked.

Boone snarled and grasped her hips in a bruising grip, pulling her back against him with every thrust. The growl turned feral as he rammed into her and froze. Pulsing jets of warmth encouraged her own explosive orgasm, and she closed her eyes against the pleasure driving through her body.

He swelled and released another hot stream into her, and she pressed back, and back farther, wanting all of him. How could anything feel this good? This right?

A deep shudder took her, shaking her shoulders as Boone strained into her again. When he pulled slowly out of her, she fought the cold that took the place of where his body had touched hers.

She was boneless, completely unable to walk or engage in any kind of competent conversation. She wanted to tell him how much she'd enjoyed that, and how much she liked being with him, but couldn't form a single word. All she could do was close her eyes and savor each deep aftershock.

Boone settled a blanket he'd tied to the backpack over the pine-needle forest floor and scooped her up, as if he knew how useless she was right now. Gently, he laid her down and pulled his jacket over them as he spooned her.

"You trusted me," he murmured against her ear.

Cora shivered at the delicious sensation of his mouth brushing her earlobe. She smiled at the gold shapes the sunlight made across the wilderness floor and snuggled back against him, reveling in the feel of his warm chest against the planes of her back. "Oh, I know you can be a dangerous man, Boone, but you'd never hurt me."

She'd spoken the words loud and clear, so he could hear how much she believed them.

His lips pressed against the back of her neck, and he smiled against the skin there. "Truth."

ELEVEN

"You're stalling," Cora accused through an unapologetic grin as she pulled her sweater over her head and straightened the hem around her hips.

"I'm not stalling, woman. I'm trying to help pack all this up so you won't have to do it." Boone clipped the rolled up blanket to his backpack and handed it to her.

"Aw, you're such a gentlebear," she said, scrunching up her nose at how cute he was.

Boone chuckled and stuffed his folded clothes into the front zipper. "You won't say that when you feel how heavy this is. I didn't think about you having to carry it after I Change." He frowned at the blue nylon material. "I think I packed too much food."

"Please," she grumbled, flexing her arm and smacking it with a kiss. "I got this."

"That's my girl."

That warm, glowing feeling threaded through her veins again, and she pulled her shoulders up to her ears in an attempt to hold another *awww* back. "I like being your girl."

Boone kissed her on the nose and sidled around to her back where he slid the straps of the pack over her shoulders.

Turning to face him, she fiddled with the camera and said, "Come on you sexy, furry bear. I want to pet you."

"Cora," Boone growled out as he hooked his hands on his hips. "I'm not a dog."

Focused on his long dick that swung with every movement of his legs, she murmured, "I can't hold a conversation when you have your trouser snake out like that."

"Trouser snake?" His lips turned up in that sexy, crooked smile she breathed for.

"Yogurt slinger."

"Cora, stop it." His grin grew brighter, though, and she didn't need that much encouragement to play this game.

Okay, now she was getting a case of the giggles. "Taco Tickler."

"All right, I'm Changing."

"Womb Raider."

"Jesus," he muttered through a laugh just before he hunched inward. His bear blasted from him in the span of a heartbeat.

The ground shook beneath her feet as Boone fell forward onto all four paws. His fur was a lot lighter than she remembered his brothers' being. It was so light it almost matched his blond hair in his human form.

"I always wanted a pet," she said in a higher pitch than she'd intended. She knew it was Boone—knew it—but that didn't stop her heart from drumming against her breastbone faster with every step he took toward her. Boone was massive. A thick muscled neck delved down to powerful legs and four inch claws that raked the earth with every movement. His eyes were that strange gold color, making him look even more inhuman, and when he opened his mouth to let off a soft grunt, his teeth were long and white and sharp as razors.

"Holy meatballs, okay." Cora froze and closed her eyes. "Don't hurt me. I didn't mean to call you a pet."

Boone bumped her backward with his oversize block head, and she grabbed the scruff of his neck instinctively to save herself from falling and blasting her tailbone through her throat. His fur wasn't as soft as she'd imagined, but instead was coarse and thick. "Oooh," she exhaled on a shaky breath. "Good werebear."

Boone snuffled his nose against her belly, tickling her, and she squirmed and laughed, expelling some of the nervousness. His ears angled back, as if he heard something, but then his eyes relaxed as he eased back and took her in.

He sat down and waited—for what, she hadn't a guess. Slowly, she approached, hand extended. "Please don't bite me."

Boone made a huffing noise in his throat.

"Are you laughing at me?"

He nodded slowly, ears forward.

Steeling her reserve, she brushed her fingertips down his chest. The fur was much softer there, so she stepped closer and ran her palm down his belly.

"Boone, Boone, you hung the moon," she sang

softly. "Is it strange that I like your bear side, too?"

He canted his giant head and shook it once, forcefully.

"Good. Now take me someplace beautiful. Someplace only you could find."

Boone swayed under her touch, then stood and strode a few paces in front. Hesitating, he looked over his shoulder, as if waiting for her.

She smiled and adjusted the viewing screen on the camera. Her hiking boots made muffled sounds as she padded through the dried pine needles to his side. Resting her hand on the giant hump between his shoulders, she walked beside him in silence, listening to the cicadas and late season birds who weren't scared off by the threat of a Colorado winter quite yet.

The hike was breathtaking, pure evergreen wilderness. She'd been excited to take the job here years ago when she'd been offered it, just to get to live in a place so beautiful. But the woods around town couldn't touch the forest here. Here, she saw things no other hiker would ever see. A willow near a creek of running water, completely private when she followed Boone into the shadows under its arching branches. A cave in a small cliff that wasn't too deep to explore entirely. Perhaps this was Boone's chosen shelter when he was in this form. But it was the scenery at the end of the trail that stole her breath away completely.

She saw it first through the screen on the video camera, thinking they were still a ways off, but when Boone stopped and looked over his massive shoulder at her, she heard it then—running water.

Mountain water tumbled down a stony cliff and created a giant cloud of mist where it hit the stream below. A beautiful waterfall, and one she would've never known existed. She stepped out of the shadow of an ancient pine tree and onto a pebbly river bank, the rocks crunching under her shoes. It would freeze soon in the winter months, but for now, it was stunning.

"Oh, Boone," she whispered reverently, afraid to disturb the magic of the place. "It's perfect. Can we eat here, on the bank?"

Boone rubbed his head down her side roughly, knocking her forward and extracting a trill of giggles from her. "Stop it, you oaf. You'll knock me into the cold river."

Hooking a powerful arm around her, Boone pulled her in against his chest and made a contented sound deep in his throat.

"Are you asking if I like your place? It's incredible, Boone. Change back so I can properly hug you. Your paws have too many weapons." Already he'd snagged a rip in her jacket.

With a grunt that sounded painful, he shrank back into his human form. His skin was pale and his flesh covered with goosebumps.

"Oh! Here," she said, pulling out his clothes from the backpack as quickly as she could manage.

"Thanks," he said in a hoarse voice.

"Are you okay?" she asked, helping tug his shirt over his head. He was tall and his muscles were twitching in waves, making her efforts clumsy at best. "That looked like it hurt a lot worse than Changing into the bear.

"Nah, I'm okay. It gets harder if I shift a lot. I just need a few minutes."

Worried, Cora rushed to lay the blanket beside the towering pine as he dressed the rest of the way. Three shifts in the last two days, and a car wreck on top of it...no wonder he was sore this time around.

Boone sat heavily, leaned against the tree bark, not bothering with shoes.

"Will food make it better?" she asked, unsure what to do.

"Yeah, but first, can you come here?"

Cora crawled over the blanket and sat in the space he'd made between his legs. Exhaling a deep sigh, Boone gathered her into his arms and pulled her tight and safe against his chest. His chin rested on her hair, and she relaxed against his warmth, watching the waterfall.

"Is this your place?" she whispered.

"My brothers and Ma and I all divvied up a large plot of land, and when we went to choose where we would put our houses, this place called to my animal. It's why I chose this part of the property. I come here when I need out of my head."

Cora pointed with the toe of her boot to something bright and red near the tree line. "Is that yours?"

"The kayak? Yeah. I'm going to take you when it warms up. The water is too cold right now, but this river has some badass scenic views."

"Now I can't wait for spring."

His deep chuckle reverberated through his chest and against her cheek. "You know, you are the most affectionate female I've ever met."

She stopped stroking his hand and looked up at him. "Does that bother you?"

"No," he answered, looking a little surprised. "With anyone else, it would make me uncomfortable, but you settle my bear. I like it when you touch me."

"What about public displays of affection? Would that bother you?"

"Like what?"

"Like holding hands when we are in town, or kissing at a street corner as we wait for a light to tell us to walk? You know, mushy stuff in front of strangers."

Boone inhaled a deep breath as his eyes tightened. "It's your public image I'd worry about then. You have a job in television. I'm pretty sure cozying up with a bear shifter would hurt people's perception of you."

"People would get over it, especially the longer bear shifters are out in the open. Someday, you'll be able to Change and walk down Main Street, and nobody will even bat an eye."

"What if that kind of acceptance doesn't come for a long time?" His eyes were serious and clear blue as he stroked her hair away from her face.

Cora sighed and rolled her head until she could see the waterfall he'd shared with her again. "Doesn't matter how long it takes, Boone. I'm not going anywhere."

TWELVE

Cora knocked softly on the production manager's office door. "Hey Mark, do you have a second?"

"Of course. I wanted to talk to you, anyway. Sit down." He rubbed his balding, shiny dome and gestured to the plush chair in front of his desk. Leaning his elbows on the desk, he clasped his hands in front of his mouth. "What's going on with you?"

"I'm sorry?"

"I mean, what was with you verbally sparring with Deanna tonight." He pushed a button on the black remote on his desk and began to play a clip of tonight's news, as if he'd had it queued up on the off-chance she stopped by his office.

She, Deanna, and Brandon were reporting on the fire in Fairplay that had taken a man's life. It was the part where they were wrapping up the segment and were allowed to converse openly. Sometimes there was a little debate during this time, but mostly they just cracked jokes they thought would appeal to the audience. Brandon, especially, was known for his one-line zingers. But tonight, Deanna had swung her gaze right to Cora and said, "It's surprising that the bear shifters aren't better at their job, what with their extra abilities and all. It's a shame the man who died was a victim of slow reaction time."

On the tape, Cora sat straight up, as if someone shocked her with the end of a live wire. "Well, *Deanna*, bear shifters are people, too, and extra strength or not, they aren't magicians. I'm sure every loss is very difficult for them, just as it would be to any other firefighter."

Deanna's eyebrows winged up nearly to her hairline, and she looked straight at the camera. "There you have it folks," she snapped. "Our hearts go out to the family of Mr. Campbell who lost his life yesterday. Have a good night."

Mark clicked the television off. "People don't like

to watch news so they can feel uncomfortable."

"No, people watch the news for current events and for honest reporting. Deanna was baiting me with the bear shifter bullshit. I talked to Boone Keller, and he was cut up about the man who died. He was there, trying to save him. Deanna is a judgmental twat who let her mouth run away with her opinion. If I get a lecture, she should be getting a slap on the wrist, too."

"And she will, but as it stands, we've been fielding disgruntled phone calls since we went off the air. We aren't a big station, Cora. If our audience leaves, we can easily be replaced by a bigger station. Hell, Denver even talks about extending this far out now. You're a fantastic reporter, and you continue to increase our audience, but you're also a bit of a loose cannon about the shifters. You've gone off script a few times now, and I've let it slide just to see where you took it. You are fantastic at finding human interest pieces, but the bear shifters are controversial, and if it looks like we're taking a side, our viewership goes down, and we can't afford that right now. Just keep it professional out there, okay?"

"So I guess this is a bad time to tell you I've

scored an interview with all of the members of the Breck Crew?"

Mark lowered his chin, his bushy gray brows lifting high. "Are you serious right now, Wright?"

"As a heart attack. But if you aren't interested in running it, I could always just upload it to my website." And then the national news stations would contact her for footage, but she didn't have to tell Mark that. He knew the sharks had been circling her since the piece she did on the bear shifters at the town hall meeting a few months ago.

Mark leaned back in his chair and rubbed that shiny head of his again, a gesture he always did when he was thinking hard about something. "When are you conducting the interviews?"

"Tomorrow during the day."

"Are you taking Carl as your cameraman?"

"Nope. The invite is just for me."

"All members?"

"Except for the cubs. The family is trying to keep them out of the spotlight as much as possible."

"Smart move."

She nodded and steadied her leg from shaking nervously. If Mark said yes to running the interviews, she could spin a positive light on the Breck Crew and make life easier on all of them.

Mark pointed to her and lowered his voice. "You run the piece by me first before it goes live. This could be what pulls audience attention and keeps those asshats from the city from vying for our territory. They're after the shifters, but if the Kellers are dealing with us exclusively, this little station just might stay on its feet. What do you need from me?"

"Access to the media room before I go home tonight. I need to pull footage of the Breck Crew from the hours we've already taped to see if I can use any of it for the feature."

"Sure, sure, that would be fine. I'll call Darla and tell her I'll be home late. I don't want you staying in the station alone."

"Aw, you worried about me, Mark?"

"Of course, I am. I heard about the wreck you were in. I pulled that story, by the way, for your privacy. Deanna wanted to run it on the news tonight. I figured you needed some time to deal with...whatever you're dealing with. Plus, if the rumors are true, the IESA was involved, and I don't really want the station going head-to-head with any of that business."

"Understood. And thank you."

"I know you were involved because of Boone Keller, Cora. Are you sure you know what you're doing?"

"Mark," she warned, frowning.

He threw his hands up. "Okay, okay, I get it. That's none of my business. Just be careful, all right? I'd hate to see you get hurt."

There was no threat in his voice, only concern, and she liked her boss even more for it.

"Boone wouldn't hurt me."

"It's not Boone I'm concerned about."

Thinking about that IESA agent right now wasn't going to fix anything, so Cora stood and straightened her black pencil skirt. "I'll be an hour in the media room, tops."

Mark rocked in his office chair and drummed the end of a pencil on his desk. "I'll be in here if you need me."

Cora left and made her way down the hallway. She waved at Brandon and told him, "Goodnight," then gathered her purse and notes from the hair and make-up room and slipped through the door at the end of the hall. The media room was her favorite place in the building, and not just because there was a vending machine that sold four separate rows of corn chips. This was a cameraman's paradise, where all of the equipment was stored and where footage could be viewed, saved, and edited. Big fluorescent lights hummed to life when she hit the switch, illuminating rows of cameras and tripods against the back cinderblock wall. She'd already told Boone she'd be a little late getting home in order to prepare for the interviews tomorrow, but when she checked her phone, there was a text that read *I'm up at the firehouse with Dade and Cody, shooting the shit. I'm not working tonight, so call me if you need anything.*

She grinned and typed in *I need werebear diddles when I get back to your place, stat.*

He replied before she was even seated in front of the trio of computer monitors in the center of the room.

Yes ma'am. Clam Wrecker.

Cora giggled and scrunched her nose as she typed the first inappropriate dick nickname that came to mind. *Leaky Meat Rod. Now stop it, I'm working.*

She tucked her phone away and entered the password on the computer, then searched for the footage of the bear shifters they had on file. So far, it wasn't much. Carl had recorded them Changing for the first time by the burning veterinary clinic when Dade had decided to Turn Quinn to save her life. And then they had a couple of hours of footage before, during, and after the town hall meeting.

She'd lied to Mark. This wasn't entirely for research. Something about what Boone had said earlier had stuck with her. He'd said he had a nightmare about her before they had even met, and she wanted to see the first moments she'd seen Boone those three months ago captured on film.

She fast forwarded through Quinn's rescue and stopped when Dade and Boone were hovering near her limp body. *Boone was wearing his fireproof turnout gear and pulled his mask off. His oxygen tank still clung to his back, and his trousers and reflective jacket were still on him, covered in soot. His eyes filled with horror at something his brother, Dade, said, and he dragged his gaze back to Quinn's body.*

"Shit," he drawled, clear as day on camera.

"What's happening?" Carl murmured.

"Just keep filming," Cora said off to the side of the shot.

Boone yanked his jacket off as Cody began to undress, too.

Cora hit fast forward for the sole purpose of skipping right over Quinn's Change, which looked horribly painful. She stopped in time to see Boone morph into the blond grizzly she'd grown to love, then hit fast forward again as that damned gunshot sounded from one of the idiots in the crowd. The bystander had shot Dade in the shoulder. She remembered that part well enough and didn't want to see it again. *The bears moved in fast motion as Quinn fought Dade and tried to charge the crowd. Cody addressed the bystanders...* There. Cora hit stop and turned up the volume on the monitor.

Cody admitted he and his brothers were bear shifters, then asked a paramedic named Greg to help Quinn. When the medic asked why Dade had bit her, Cora stepped from her hiding spot behind the fire engine.

She advised him, "Don't answer any more questions. I think you should think carefully about the things that come from your mouth right now. An informal interview will only hurt you when emotions are running high like this. Plus, your brother has been shot." Carl had recorded her back as she pointed to Dade.

"Who are you?" Cody asked.

"I work for the news. I'll break this story if you want me to, but I think we need to take a step back."

Cora leaned forward, straining her eyes at the grainy screen where Boone's bear stood. He moved, just slightly.

She rewound the tape and played it again. Then again to make sure she wasn't imagining it. Zooming in, she played it one last time. There it was, unmistakable. *He swayed on his feet the moment he laid eyes on her, then took a step toward her and shook his head, as if he hadn't told his body to do that.*

"What the hell?" She tried to remember seeing Boone. She recalled everything from that day so clearly, but her focus had been on Cody, who looked like the leader. That and trying not to get the rest of the bear shifters shot by the dumbass waving the handgun behind her.

She saved that stretch of tape to a blue thumb drive she kept on her keychain, then searched with shaking fingers for the tape of the town hall meeting. She couldn't get to it fast enough to calm her racing heart. She scoured the footage of the Kellers arriving at the town hall. Carl hadn't recorded any footage of Boone as they'd made their way into the meeting. Nothing but his back as he walked with his crew to sit in front of the Mayor, City Council, and the full hall.

Boone sat down in a row with the rest of the Breck Crew, and his nostrils flared as he seemed to look everywhere but at her.

She fast forwarded through Cody's speech and stopped at the part where Dade stood.

"Some bear shifters go their entire lives without the urge to settle on one mate," Dade explained, "and then some of us are lucky enough to form a bond."

Cora gasped and hit the pause button on Boone's face, eyes frozen on where she had stood beside the camera. His sad expression made her guts go frigid. She rewound the footage and watched it again. Yes, right there! He had looked at her just after Dade talked about the bond.

The bond.

She hit play again. In the next sequence of footage, a man asked Cody if a bear shifter would force a relationship with a woman that he formed a bond with. *Boone looked furious as he stood and answered. "Absolutely not. Women in our culture are revered and make their own decisions. If they don't feel the bond, it's their choice to tell us to fuck off."*

Boone had bonded to her, of that she was sure. That's why he had nightmares of something awful happening to her that he couldn't protect her from. That's why he hadn't been able to stay away from her, though he'd obviously tried.

Why hadn't he just said that?

Was he waiting to see if she felt it, too?

Or was keeping this secret Boone's way of giving him an out in case he wanted to push her away again?

She saved the recording to her thumb drive and shoved away from the desk. Chest heaving, she stared at a frozen shot of Boone staring sadly at her. He'd thought they would never be together then. Already, before he even met her, he'd planned on staying away from her.

She was angry, shaken, and frustrated, then hopeful, and then angry all over again.

He should've told her.

After she yanked her cell from her purse, she

punched in *I'm on my way back to your house*, then hit send.

Boone Leland Keller, keeper of too many secrets, had some serious explaining to do.

THIRTEEN

There was a motorcycle parked in front of Boone's house—one of those big, loud, black and chrome numbers. She parked her Outback next to it and dragged in a big, steadying breath before she opened the door and slid out. The bike must be how Boone was getting around with his truck in the shop. Motorcycles had always scared her for the danger factor, but he was a damned bear shifter who had healed from internal injuries in a day. What was a little road rash to a shifter? Nope, she couldn't worry about his safety on a motorcycle right now. Not when her nerves were making her feel lightheaded like this.

"Boone?" she asked in a pitchy voice as she opened the front door. Clearing her throat, she scanned the empty living room and tried again. "Are you here?"

"Yeah." His voice sounded garbled. "I'm in the bathroom."

Cora tossed her purse on the couch and peeled out of her high heels before she padded into his bathroom.

Boone was leaning over the sink, flaxen hair in damp tendrils in front of his face as he brushed his teeth, half-naked. A thick, white towel was slung low on his hips.

He spat and rinsed, then grinned at her in the mirror. Slowly, he turned and leaned back on the sink. "Damn, Trouble. You're a sight for sore eyes." His smile ticked and faltered. Straightening, he asked, "What's wrong?"

"Why didn't you tell me about the bond?"

Boone froze, like a picturesque statue that belonged in some stately garden. Two heartbeats, and he leaned back against the counter again, scrubbing his hand down his face.

"What do you want to know?"

"Are you bonded to me?"

He licked his lips and angled his face away from

her. "Cora, it's not that simple."

"It is. Yes or no. One or the other. Have you bonded to me?"

His throat worked as he swallowed. Dragging his gaze to her, he nodded once.

"I saw it. The moment you laid eyes on me at the vet clinic fire, that's when it first happened, wasn't it? And then you gave it away at the town meeting when Dade was talking about the bond. You looked right at me. Me. Why me? Why did your bear choose me?"

Boone's eyes rimmed with moisture, and he averted his gaze, hiding his emotion from her. "You mean, why did my bear curse you? I don't know. I don't. It's not magic. It's science. I'd seen you a hundred times on the news and thought you were pretty, but that was it. Then I saw you in person, and my damned bear was done. I couldn't think about anything else."

"Why didn't you introduce yourself then?"

"You were dating someone."

"Did you know I was dating someone?"

"No."

"Explain this to me so I understand what it is we're really doing here. This feels big—huge! Why didn't you tell me you'd bonded to me?"

"You want to know why?" he gritted out, brushing past her into his room. He yanked the top drawer to his bedside table open and grabbed a handful of envelopes. With a flick of his wrist, he threw them across the bed. "That's why, Cora. Some of these are death threats. The others are job offers from the biggest, baddest underground mafias, mobs, and drug runners. And those aren't even all of them. I've shredded a couple hundred, and the rest has gone to Cody, Gage, and Dade. Some even come to Ma. This is your future with me. I'm still an assassin for hire, Cora."

"You aren't."

"I am what they think I am!" His face had morphed into something heartbreaking—anger and defeat, sadness and a plea for her to accept the monster inside of him. "Whatever the world thinks of you, that's what you are. It's why your public image is so important. Surely, *you* can see that."

"They don't know you yet, Boone. If they saw the man I see, they'd let us be. They'd respect you. And pushing me away because of this?" She scooped up a trio of letters and tossed them at his chest. "That's bullshit."

"I'm here, aren't I? I gave in to my need for you. What else do you want from me?"

"Everything! Full disclosure. I should know what I'm in. You bonded to me, and I thought we were just dating."

"We are just dating. I'm not asking for more."

"And what about when I want more? Is this your cutoff point? Is there a future for us, Boone?"

He sat heavily on the bed and buried his face in his hands. "I don't know."

"Wrong answer. The answer you meant to say is fuck yes, Cora, I want you, I'm bonded to you, I can see how much you love me—"

Boone jerked his head up and muttered, "Don't say that."

"It's true! I love you." A sob escaped her throat, and her shoulders sagged as she held her hands out, palms up. "You should've just told me and left the choice up to me whether to stay in this or not. Boone." She waited for him to say something— anything—but he didn't. "Boone, you have to talk to me."

"I am my father, Cora. I'm going to ruin you, ruin

your life, ruin your career." A single tear slid down his cheek, and he gritted his teeth and wiped it on his shoulder. "What happens when we realize I inherited the same fucked up, broken bond my dad had with Ma for all those years? What happens when I fuck up, or worse? What happens if you get hurt because of what I am? I didn't tell you about the bond because I wanted to give you the option of walking away from this, guilt free."

"Am I it for you?"

Boone made a ticking sound and jerked his gaze away from her. "Don't ask me that."

"Am I it for you?" she repeated louder as she crossed her arms.

"Yes," he whispered.

"Boone Leland Keller, you are not your father. He made his mistakes, and I'm sorry that broke your faith in him and your faith in yourself. But his bad decisions aren't genetic. You are a good man. Look at me." She sank down onto the mattress beside him and slid her hand against his cheek, pulled his gaze to her. "You're a *good man*. Being bonded to me isn't a bad thing. It's not. I'm in this with you."

"But what if—"

"What if we just had tonight? Tomorrow will take care of itself, and none of it is in our control. But I'd rather have one great day with you than a thousand forgettable days with someone else."

Boone's face crumpled as he crushed her to him. He buried his face against her neck and held her so tightly, it was hard to breathe. The discomfort was worth it, though, because right now, she could feel Boone opening up, letting her through the cinderblock walls he'd carefully built around his heart.

The world didn't know Boone yet. Didn't know how good he was, or how funny, or how gentle and sensitive he could be despite the animal inside of him. They didn't know how much he loved his family, or how protective he was of his loved ones, or how adored he was.

She hugged him tighter and squeezed her eyes closed as he rocked them slowly back and forth.

If it was the last thing she did, she was going to show the world how wrong it was about Boone.

FOURTEEN

Fury blasted through Cora's veins as she screeched and gripped her steering wheel in a choke hold. Eddie, that sniveling nard-face, had done the unspeakable.

Cora pulled to a stop at a red light on Main Street and glared at the newspaper sitting in her passenger seat. He'd singled her out, writing an article naming her the "Human Consort of the Breck Crew." It was right under a picture of her and Boone at the bar standing close and gazing into each other's eyes. Sure, they'd possibly been arguing in that picture, but it sure as sugar tits looked like a passionate exchange of sweet nothings from where she sat. But worse than that—so much worse than that—Eddie had called the

Breck Crew a "family of trained liars" and ran an article quoting Cody at the town meeting.

The quote he pulled said, "We bond with one mate for life. The rate of infidelity for bear shifters is almost none because our animals simply won't allow it." Then Eddie had outed Titus Keller's affair and secret child, raised away from Boone's family until the age of ten. Bruiser's story had made the front page of the small town newspaper.

It made her sick. Not only had her ex basically called her 'Whore of the Wearbear,' but he'd made a really painful and personal family affair public.

This was all her fault for not answering Eddie's stupid one billion text messages and calls over the last few weeks. She hadn't wanted to hear anything he had to say, but never in a hundred years would she have guessed he would stoop this low to hurt her.

And now "liar" had been added to the public's perception of the bear shifters. She didn't know how it would affect them on a national level, but in a small town like Breckenridge, reputation was everything.

"Asshole," she groused as she pulled into a small parking lot behind Jos's candy store.

She had to make this right, and the only one she

knew to ask for help was her cousin.

Snatching the newspaper from the seat, Cora slid out of her car, then slammed the door hard enough to rock it.

"Hey," Jos greeted her as Cora blew through the front door. Today, her short black hair was tied back with a white bandana, and her navy apron was dusted with flour and drizzled with chocolate. "Let me see it."

Unable to express the anger she felt with words, Cora handed her the newspaper and sank into a chair behind the counter as Jos glared at the tiny newsprint, lips moving as she read along silently. Every once in a while, Jos's eyebrows would shoot up, and she'd huff air in that sonofabitch-really-did-it-now kind of way Cora recognized from when Jos had protected her from bullies in high school back in Denver.

Meredith came out of the back room and asked the lone customer in the store if he needed help finding anything but returned to Cora's side when he responded that he was just looking around. Meredith was a study in opposites from Jos. Fair skin, perfectly highlighted blond hair pulled into a ponytail that curled just right on the end, and manners. Cora had never heard her cuss as long as she'd known her.

"Hey sweetie," Meredith said, giving Cora a side-hug.

"I want to punch that little weasel in his little weasel throat," Jos gritted out, handing the paper to Meredith. She swung her gaze back to Cora and exclaimed, "Like he didn't hurt you enough already!"

"Well, he actually did me a favor by cheating because I finally grew the balls to leave him and find someone better. Someone who makes me better."

"Oh, honey, it'll all be okay," Meredith said, sympathy pooling in her soft green eyes.

"It will because we're going to slash his tires and poop on his porch," Jos growled.

"Okay, first off, you put dog poop on the porch. You don't actually pop a squat and defecate, and second, I've already got a better idea."

"A plan?"

Cora lifted her chin, and then lowered it with a sigh. "Yes, I've got a plan. But I need your help."

"Name it. Anything."

"I've been approved by Mark, my producer, to run the interviews I did with the Breck Crew yesterday by him so he can put it on the air. He's given me a fifteen minute time slot to run right before I do the news tonight."

"Okay, I'm with you. Where do I come in?"

"Well, okay, let me show you." Cora pulled her handheld video camera from her purse and hit play. It was tape of her hand gripping Boone's fur as he led her through the woods. The camera panned up as Boone stopped, and he looked back at her with such adoration in his blazing gold eyes. The sun filtered through the trees with yellow saturated light, and the evergreen woods behind him were a spectacular backdrop, but it was the look of utter devotion in Boone's eyes that made her feel all breathy. It was one of Cora's favorite parts of the tape.

"Oh, my gosh," Jos and Meredith murmured in unison.

"That's Boone?" Jos asked, looking up at Cora with emotion-filled eyes.

"That's my Boone," she whispered.

"How much footage did you get?"

"I've videotaped over the last couple of days, sometimes with just me and Boone, and then all yesterday when I was with his family."

"Is the candid footage of his family like this?"

Cora swallowed her emotions down and nodded. "They're lovely. Everything I could want in a family. Ma, Rory, Leah, Quinn, the cubs...the Keller brothers. They even turned the interview questions on me sometimes, and Ma asked me to stay for dinner, and I got footage of that, too. I didn't think about adding my personal video sequences to the interview until I saw the newspaper today. The world should see this amazing family for what it is. So, my question for you is, do you remember how to use any of the editing software from when we used to do those documentaries in college?"

"Oh, geez, I'll be rusty, but we can give it a go. How much time do we have?"

"I have to have the thumb drive to Mark by five."

Jos looked at her watch. "Okay, we've got roughly eight hours to give you enough time to get back to the station. I'm in," Jos said suddenly. "It's a really good thing you are doing."

"It's a risky thing I'm doing. It could cost me my job, my career."

"Cora, this feels big, and right." Jos grabbed her hands. "You can help these people."

"Yeah. Even if Mark caves under the backlash, I have this one chance to make sure the public sees the real Breck Crew, not some made-up rumors like Eddie wants them to see."

"My name goes on the credits," Jos negotiated.

"Done, and so will yours Meredith."

"But I'm not doing anything," Meredith said, looking baffled.

"Yeah, you are babe. You're watching the shop all on your own today while I help Cora edit this. Is that okay?"

Meredith laughed as Jos kissed her nose and bolted for the door, then Meredith called out, "Anything for a good cause."

"Thank you," Cora whispered, hugging Meredith up tight. She waved with a nervous flutter of her fingertips as she followed Jos out the back door.

Eddie thought she'd cave with embarrassment at being labeled as Boone's consort, but he was dead fuckin' wrong.

She was about to own exactly who she was and where she belonged.

FIFTEEN

Boone shrugged out of his turnout gear and kicked out of his trousers. It was cold as a witch's tit outside, but he had been burning up inside that fireproof jacket. That damned newspaper article was messing with his head. Poor Ma. She'd been through hell dealing with his father's secret infidelity, and now she'd have to bear that shame in front of the whole town any time she went anywhere. Yeah, when Bruiser had turned up at age ten, the rumors had swirled out of control about their family, but that had settled years ago, and now, everyone knew his father was a two-timing asshole for sure.

And on top of that, Cora's ex had called her Boone's consort on the first page. Fuck, he wanted to rip that idiot's throat out and watch him gasp on every last breath. Boone jammed his hat on the hook near his locker and cast a baleful glance over his shoulder at the engine that needed a wash down. At least today he would stay busy.

He'd called Cora as soon as he read the article, but she'd seemed more concerned with how he was handling the news on his father. Damn, he wished he was off today so he could leave and check on her. She'd said she was working all day, though, so a day off wouldn't get him any more time with her, anyway. Still, he'd give his right femur to hug his mate right now and make sure she was really okay.

It was this grit right here that had made him keep the bond to himself. Cora was a good woman, a stubborn, strong, proud woman, who was loyal to a fault. At least if she hadn't known he was bonded to her, she could've gone her own way if things got too hard. She was smart though, quick as a whip, and had figured out immediately how important being bonded was.

She wouldn't quit on him.

That realization made him hook his hands on his hips and huff a breath. He nodded slowly as he let that little gem slide over him. His mate was no quitter, especially when it came to handling his many demons.

She really was in this, like she'd said, and how the hell Boone had been lucky enough to snag a woman like her, he didn't have a clue. He just needed to thank his sheer dumb luck and do his best to make her as happy as she made him.

His phone chirped from his back pocket, and he rushed to answer it in case it was Cora.

He grinned when he saw her name on his caller ID. "Hey, Trouble," he answered.

"Are you at the firehouse, or are you out on a call?" she asked in a low voice.

"I'm at the firehouse, why?"

"Call your Ma and Leah and the others, and gather those boys because your interview is coming on in five minutes."

"Wha—already? You just did them yesterday."

"Tight deadline."

"Damn, woman, you work fast. Okay, I'll let everyone know. Are you still working tonight?"

"Yes, I'll be reporting the news directly after the interviews."

"Okay, I can't wait to see you on there."

She giggled, but it was a nervous sound. "Hey, Boone?"

"Yeah?" he asked stifling the nervous spark that had ignited in his gut.

"No matter what, I love you."

No matter what? "I love you, too. Hey, is there something I'm missing here? Are you okay?"

"Yes, yes, I'm fine. I just...I just hope you like the segment. Oh, my producer is here and I still need to go through hair and make-up. I'll see you tonight. Call the crew! Okay, bye."

Boone frowned at the screen until it turned off from the ended call. She was acting strange. Maybe the interviews hadn't gone as well as he'd thought they did.

"Gage, Cody, Dade, come in here." He'd called them out at a normal volume, but his brothers would hear well enough. "Jimmy and Barret, you might as well come, too," he said, gesturing to a couple of human firefighters working this shift.

Boone dialed Ma's number as he turned on the television in the rec room. "Ma, turn it on channel four. Cora said our interviews are coming up in a few minutes."

"They are? Leah, turn the TV to channel four. Cora is showing our interviews. Oh, I have to go, Boone. I have to make popcorn for the cubs, or they'll never sit still long enough for us to watch."

"What is it?" Cody asked as Boone hung up on Ma.

"Call your mates and tell them the interviews are about to come on."

"When?" Dade asked.

"Right now. Gage, Leah already knows. She's over at Ma's house with the cubs."

His oldest brother nodded and jogged off toward the kitchen.

"Where are you going?"

"Snacks, man," Gage called over his shoulder. He was still wearing his hat and suspenders and Boone chuckled at how easily distracted his oldest brother was.

Channel four was currently running a commercial for some heavy-duty cleaner that could dissolve rust off nails. The acidic solution reminded him of what the tracker had done to Dade's neck and Cody's hand and made him wince as he sat down.

Jimmy and Barret took the smaller couch while Cody and Dade hovered on the arms of the bigger one with him. Gage came in with a bag of trail mix and sat down practically in Boone's lap.

"Personal space, man," Boone grumbled, shoving his brother over.

Gage clunked his boot onto the coffee table and shoved a handful of peanuts and raisins into his mouth. He only ever ate those two things from the mix, leaving the filler for the rest of them to eat, the peckerwood.

The intro for the local news came on, and Dade sang along, hitting every note.

Boone rolled his eyes and leaned forward, elbows on his knees. "Damn, I'm nervous."

"Why? It's not like she can make us look any worse," Dade said.

"True." Cody yanked the bag of snacks from Gage's hands.

Jimmy narrowed his eyes at the screen and relaxed into the couch cushions. "If you called us in here just to watch your girlfriend on TV—"

"Shhh," the Keller brothers all hissed as Brandon Musgrave came on.

"Tonight, we have a special treat for you. As many of you know, just three short months ago our world was rocked with the discovery that human-animal shifters, bear shifters in particular, have been existing alongside man all this time. Well tonight, our very own Cora Wright has got the exclusive interviews you've been dying to see. World, meet the Breck Crew in a piece she's calling *An Authentic Look into the Secret Lives of Bear Shifters*. Whew, that title is a mouthful..."

"Shut uuup," Gage drawled, tossing a cashew at the flat screen.

The reporter cracked another stupid joke, and Boone snickered when the screen cut to black right in the middle of his punchline. That's what he got, screen hog.

The black screen transitioned to an image of the day the Breck Crew had come out publicly in front of the veterinary clinic. Of how scared Quinn looked when she Changed for the first time. They were black and white Polaroid pictures stacked on top of one another, the top disappearing as another image appeared to evoke even more emotion. They were gritty, grainy.

Cody holding his hands out as he talked to the

crowd.

Dade looking at Boone as he stripped off his turnout gear.

The crowd terrified, hiding behind the fire engine.

Newspaper headlines passed in rapid succession, some for shifters, some against.

Video of riots nationally, as well as on Main Street, flowed seamlessly together, showing some of the harsher signs, encouraging the government to keep them in cages, then morphing to signs of hope. The Blue Haired Ladies of Breckenridge stood in one shot, holding up a sign that simply read Let Them Be.

Frightened faces in a crowd.

A mother clutching onto her child.

Video of the Breck Crew walking up the steps of town hall. One shot showed people reaching out to touch Ma's outstretched hand, while on the other side, a man threw a rock at them.

This was the first time Boone had thought about how confusing this must've been for the humans. How scary it must've been to realize they weren't the only ones making a life on this planet. Their coming out had caused such uncertainty and chaos, but it wasn't because they were evil people. It was because humans were scared.

Shaky video of the night of the wreck appeared, trained on sparkling shards of window glass that sat like shining gemstones on Cora's trembling hand. The IESA agent's voice rang out loud and clear over Cora's ragged breath. "They're still breathing. Nah, there's no cameras on this street. No houses either. I picked it carefully. Yeah, I said I'll take care of it, and I will. I'll call you when it's done."

A scuffle, and a terrified scream from Cora's throat, then the camera trained on a syringe that landed on the seat right next to her.

"You stupid animal," the man growled from the concrete where Boone pinned him. "You were the warning, you and your whore. The rest of your crew would've come back in line." The video threaded, shortening the fight, highlighting the poison the IESA agent had spewed. "If you kill me, it won't matter. There will be someone new to take my place, but you already know that. We're going to eradicate your kind until you are nothing but a dim memory. You didn't play by our rules, and now there will be consequences. You thought coming out to the public made you safer? Look in those people's eyes. They hate you. Hate what

you stand for. IESA was the only thing that could've kept you safe."

The camera focused on the attackers sneering crimson smile, then faded to the interview room Cora had set up in Ma's house.

"What do you see in your future?" Cora asked Cody. She wore a crisp, white sleeveless blouse and dark, fitted skirt as she sat in a chair across from the couch Cody sat in. The backdrop was Ma's living room wall, covered in family pictures.

"I don't see my future at all. As alpha, I worry for my crew. Where will we be in ten years? I don't know. I don't know if we'll be here past next week. Where do I wish our future would end up? I hope my family is safe, and that my mate is happy. I hope my Ma can take her grandkids to the playground without worrying that someone will take their kids away so they don't play with our cubs. I hope my brothers are happy with their mates and that we continue serving this great community of ours. I hope we're living in peace."

"And what do you see for your son, Aaron?"

Cody's face crumpled, and he jerked his head away toward the shadows. He tried to smile apologetically, but faltered and shook his head. "Sorry," he said in a thick voice. "My son just came into my life, so this is hard to talk about. Can we redo this?"

"Of course, just answer when you are ready and I can edit it."

Cody leaned forward and clasped his hands in front of his face. "Why is she using the outtakes?"

"Because," Boone whispered, jerking his head toward Jimmy and Barret, whose attention was glued to the screen. "Cora's not going for perfect. She's going for real and relatable."

Boone swung his gaze back to the screen. Damn. Even he was choking up watching Cody get emotional over his boy.

The next interview brought some levity to the heavy subject matter.

Ma sat next to Leah, Rory, and Quinn on the couch across from Cora.

"What was your biggest fear about coming out to the public?" Cora asked.

Ma squeezed Leah's leg and sat up straight and proud. "I was scared they were going to split us up—"

"Grammy!" Aaron called from out of the camera shot somewhere.

"I was afraid—" Ma tried again, trying to hide an

indulgent smile.

"Bacon," Aaron called. "I wanted waffles and bacon, and me and Arie and Tate were going to make enough for you, but I can't find the bacon anywhere."

Leah, Rory, and Quinn were all pursing their lips, shoulders shaking as they tried to stifle their laughter. Quinn snorted, and it was all over as they burst into a fit of giggles.

"I was afraid they would split up my family, but Aaron over here, my five-year-old grandson, is only concerned with the bacon shortage in this house. Boy, I told you I have to go to the grocery store, and even if we did have bacon, you can't cook it yourself. The stove isn't a toy. Now shut that fridge door before you let all the cold air out." *Ma shook her head at something off camera.* "No popsicles. Those are for treats."

Rory spoke up. "Aaron, we're doing an interview. You were supposed to be good and play in the toy room with your cousins, remember?"

"I want to be on television." *Aaron's voice got louder with every word. Suddenly, a giant blue eyeball appeared right in the screen, and he whispered,* "Hi," *against the microphone.*

Now not even Cora could keep her composure as

she pulled the tot into her lap and tickled him. "Take five."

The next several minutes were a mashup of moments Cora must've caught on film yesterday. The family around Ma's dining table, playing a board game, trash-talking and over-celebrating. The Crew sitting on the front porch eating spaghetti from paper bowls, the laughter and murmured conversation constant. Boone playing with the cubs and pretending all three of them had overpowered him on the front lawn. Rory's toes tucked under Cody's legs as he stroked her hair and talked to Dade. Ma's look of sheer pride when Gage picked his cubs up and covered them with biting kisses as they laughed and laughed. Dade dancing with Quinn in the kitchen when they were doing dishes and thought no one was watching. Quinn's bare feet were on top of Dade's scuffed up old work boots, her dress swishing around her knees as she smiled against his chest.

Endless moments Boone hadn't even realized were so profound, but Cora had seen it with that special way she viewed the world. In awe of what she'd done, he wiped his hand over the two day scruff on his face.

She interviewed them all, but only the real moments were included. The mess-ups and the tears. The quivering lips and the looks of adoration as they talked about the crew they loved. The instances where their human sides were on display.

Boone's heart sank when the clip transitioned to him, looking unsettled on the couch, because he already knew which clip she had chosen.

"Boone," Cora said softly with a shy smile.

"Cora," he said, leaning forward just to be closer to her.

"You like me."

"Trouble, that isn't a question."

"Do you like me?"

His smile faded, then returned, sadder this time. "I love you." Draping his arm over the couch, he sighed deeply and shook his knee in a fast, nervous rhythm.

"What do you see for our future?"

He shook his head. "I don't want to do this on camera."

"Fine, it's just you and me. What are we?"

He leaned forward again and ran his hands through his hair. "You're my mate. You're everything. What we have when we're together feels like...everything that's good."

"Someday, would you consider Turning me so I could be like you? So I could be bound as your mate by shifter tradition?"

Boone shook his head for a long time, dragged his gaze to Cora, then away.

She sat stoically, waiting.

"No," he said finally.

"If I wanted to be a part of this crew, and if we loved each other enough, why wouldn't you want to make me like you?"

He grimaced, muscles twitching around his clenched teeth. "Because I don't want this for you. I want you to be happy. I don't want people to think you're a monster."

Cora dragged tear-rimmed eyes, openly hurt by their reality, to the camera. Slowly, she stood and approached the lens and the screen went black as she turned it off.

The next sequence was of shots she'd taken when he was a bear, leading her to his waterfall.

Hands in his fur, him gazing back at her like she was the whole sun and sky.

"Boone, Boone, you hung the moon," she sang, but

she was wrong. She was the one who hung the moon. The moon and the stars and everything that mattered.

"Is it strange that I like your bear side, too?" she asked.

His bear shook his head. Of course, it wasn't strange.

"Now take me someplace beautiful. Someplace only you could find," she murmured off camera as the lens stayed focused on him.

The final shot was the waterfall. She turned the camera on them, resting against the huge pine near the bank, smiling like nothing could touch them in those woods. He looked relaxed and happy, so different from the beginning shots of him right after coming out to the public. Cora giggled and turned the camera back on the mist under the waterfall.

The scene faded to nothing and the credits began to roll.

The room was dead silent as they stared at the white lettering across the screen.

"Holy shit," Jimmy muttered.

Cody grabbed Boone's shoulder and shook him. Gage and Dade were now clapping slowly, and this feeling of such overwhelming emotion was sitting so heavy on Boone's chest, it was hard to breathe.

Dade's phone rang, and he burst into a shit-eating grin as soon as he answered it. "Quinn's crying. She says they're all crying."

"Well?" Cody asked, brows arched high at Boone. "What are you going to do about this?"

Boone nodded slowly and grinned up at his brother, his alpha. "I'm gonna go get my girl."

"Damn straight you are. Load up! We're going on a grocery run."

"We don't need groceries," Jimmy argued.

"Dumbass," Dade said. "That's code for get in the engine. We all have to stay together while we're on shift, and Boone needs to go see Cora."

"Oh, right." Jimmy lurched up and yelled for shotgun.

Cody blasted the siren as he sped down Main Street toward the news station just outside of town. By the time they pulled up, Boone was just about driven mad with the need to hold his mate.

His mate.

Damn, how had he gotten so lucky?

He was out before Cody pulled the engine to a stop. As soon as his boots hit the pavement, he bolted up the steps, headed straight for the news station's front door.

He'd been here on a fire inspection before but didn't remember exactly where the studio room was. Inhaling deeply, he followed the scent of strawberries and mint, bustling past people who made shocked noises.

There she was. Lights bright on her as she sat behind a long podium with the other news anchors. She was talking through a smile, but her eyes were puffy, as if she'd been crying, and her cheeks had gone all rosy. Weaving through the bystanders, he ignored the man with a clipboard and earphones who called out, "Hey, we're live. You can't go up there!"

"Keep rolling," a stout man with glasses and a bald head ordered.

Cora stood, her perfect lips hanging open in shock when she saw him. "Boone?"

He jogged up the stairs to get to her and crushed her to him as soon as he reached her, lifting her off the ground. She was laughing, and crying, and hugging him around his neck.

He opened his eyes and waved an apology to Brandon and Deanna, the other anchors. Deanna was wiping tears from the corners of her eyes with a damp tissue.

"Trouble, you can have all of me."

"What do you mean?"

"I mean everything. A ring if you want it, a bear. I'll claim you if it's what you want. I was scared of hurting you, but you're strong enough. You're strong enough."

Twin shining tears streaked down her cheeks as she pressed her lips against his, then covered his face with tiny kisses. Easing back, she searched his face. "Well, Boone, are you going to ask me proper or what?"

"One knee!" Dade called out from the shadows.

"One knee!" a bunch of voices he didn't recognize echoed.

"Yeah, all right, all right." Boone dropped to his knee. "Cora," he said, taking her hands in his. "I don't have a ring to put on your finger yet, but I will."

"Here," Deanna said, handing him a tissue box.

"Thanks," he murmured, pulling one out. He rolled it into a line and wrapped it around Cora's ring finger. "The real one will be shinier, I promise."

Cora laughed thickly and dashed the back of her

hand over her damp lashes as she sniffled.

"Cora," he said, his heart drumming against his ribcage as he looked up into her beautiful, heart-shaped face and open, adoring hazel eyes. "To me, you're already my mate, but I want you to be more than that. I want my last name on you, and I want you to feel like you belong in the Breck Crew. I'd be honored if you allowed me to claim you. Cora Wright, will you marry me?"

A tiny, adorable-as-shit squeak wrenched from her throat, and she nodded, her chin bobbing double time.

"Is that a yes?"

Her smile turned megawatt as she laughed and looked around at the crowd that had gathered just outside the stage lighting. Some of them were already clapping.

Cora shook her head as if she couldn't believe she was in this moment with him. "That's a hell yes."

EPILOGUE

"Here, let me," Quinn said softly, taking the eyeliner pencil from Cora's hand.

"I don't know why I'm shaking so badly," Cora said on a breath. "I'm so ready for this."

"Are you nervous about tonight?" Rory asked, adjusting the strap of her cream-colored, lace inlay gown. "Because that, I completely understand. I have to pee every half an hour just thinking about it."

"Neither one of you should be nervous about Cody and Boone Turning you," Quinn said as she applied a steady black line over Cora's lashes. "It only hurts for a minute, and then it's wonderful. You get to meet your bears tonight."

Cora got all choked up thinking about how far

they'd all come. Today, all three would take the Keller name, and after Cora and Rory were Turned tonight, the Breck Crew would be complete.

Leah looked up from Cora's ivory dress, pulled the last pin out of her mouth, and tucked in the last piece of beaded fabric before fastening it into place. Thank goodness for her seamstress skills because there hadn't been enough time to get the strapless, fitted dress altered, and Cora had been having nightmares about tripping over it and ruining the ceremony for everyone. True, it was a laid back affair, as they had all agreed they wanted, but still.

"There you go. All hemmed and perfect," Leah said, shaking her curled dark hair over her shoulder and smiling brightly. "Are you all ready?"

Cora looked expectantly at Quinn and Rory, both gorgeous in their gowns. They nodded.

Outside the door, Ma waited with bouquets of late season roses in soft pinks. She was already crying, so Cora hugged her shoulders and told her, "Ma, you're going to get me all weepy."

"No, dear, you'll ruin your make-up. They are tears of joy. I couldn't have handpicked better mates for my boys. You've all made me so proud." She turned and pulled her fifth daughter-in-law to her side. "You too, Diem."

Bruiser's wife blushed and smiled shyly, then held out her hand. On her palm sat three strawberry-shaped sapphire hair pins. "Strawberries for the Keller mark, and the color for something blue. A gift from my father and me."

"Oh, Diem," Cora said, reverently touching one. "They're beautiful."

"May I?" she asked.

Cora bent, allowing a better angle for Diem to place the pin in the curled hair gathered in back.

"I like the pink dye in your hair," Diem said in a soft voice, touching the pinned lock gently.

Cora laughed and stood, admiring Diem's sparkling gift in a hallway mirror. "I think I'm going to keep the color for a while. It suits me now."

Ma fussed over Cora's necklace as Diem placed the pins in Rory and Quinn's hair in turn. And when at last they were ready, they moved toward the double doors where Monroe was waiting for them. The police officer dipped his chin and touched the bill of his hat, then opened the barrier wide.

A city hall marriage might not be the most

romantic locale, but it suited Cora just fine. She was getting more than a husband today. She was sharing this momentous time in her life with women who had become like sisters to her. She was gaining a family with the words she would recite to Boone here today.

Squeezing Rory and Quinn's hands, she kissed Ma on the cheek and gave Diem and Leah a smile and a wink.

With a deep breath, she looked down the aisle, and her gaze collided with Boone's. His answering smile pulled her closer, step by step until she stood in front of him.

Tagan James, alpha of the Ashe Crew and personal friend to Bruiser, had been ordained and had agreed to preside over their marriages. It seemed fitting that a stranger didn't do it, and instead, the same man who married Diem and Bruiser now bonded the other Kellers with their mates here today.

The alpha's piercing blue eyes scanned the couples, Rory and Cody, Quinn and Dade, and finally, she and Boone.

Cora looked up into Boone's clear, happy eyes, and her heart melted at how relaxed and well-rested he was now. Big changes had happened when they stopped fighting their destinies, and one of those was that his nightmares had stopped.

Boone shook his head in awe as he dragged his gaze over her dress. *You're so beautiful*, he mouthed.

Grinning, she slid her hands into his as Tagan began the ceremony. It was short and sweet, just as they'd wanted it. Traditional vows repeated together as the cubs fidgeted and giggled near Ma. Bruiser and Gage stood for the men, and Leah and Diem for the women.

It was simple and perfect, and when Tagan announced that the Kellers could kiss their brides, Cora's stomach did flip-flops with how handsome her mate—her husband—was in his pressed suit with that sexy smile just for her. He leaned forward and touched her lips with his before cupping her cheek and brushing his tongue gently against her mouth.

God, this feeling—she loved the way Boone loved her.

There were tears, so many joyous tears, and embracing and laughter. And just as Cora thought life couldn't get any better than right here in this moment, Cody led them outside.

Cora's heart sank when she saw the handful of

protestors with their cruel signs, but Boone ignored them and scooped her up, then walked right past them as if he didn't see them at all.

"I have a surprise for you," he whispered against her ear.

She wrapped her arms around his neck, clutching her flowers between his shoulder blades. "I love surprises."

Boone jerked his chin and waited as she took in the decorated fire engine. *Just Married* it said across one of the windows, and behind was tied tin cans and white streamers. Already, the cubs were scrambling up the back with Bruiser and Gage. The rest of them piled in the front two bench seats, sitting on laps and giggling in fits. Cody drove, blasting the horn and siren.

Cora looked out the window, shocked at the chaos that reined Main Street of their small mountain town. "What's happening?" she asked, utterly baffled.

"Look," Boone said, pointing.

Hung across the street was a huge, white banner. *Congratulations to the Breck Crew.*

And everywhere, people were cheering. Cody pulled to a stop and turned to them. "Welcome to your reception."

Rory and Quinn's mouths dropped open, matching Cora's. In the crowd were smiling faces. These people weren't here to protest their marriages. They were here to celebrate them.

Cora's eyes blurred with tears as Boone helped her down from the fire engine. "I don't understand."

"It was your documentary," Boone said, hugging her against his side and smiling at the gatherers. "It sparked something in people—something incredible." He looked down at her and kissed her forehead. "You once said that someday bear shifters would walk Changed in the streets, and no one would bat an eye. We aren't there yet, but I know that someday, we will be."

In disbelief, she looked over the throngs of onlookers. Jos and Meredith were there, waving and cheering. The Blue Haired Ladies, Mark, Deanna, and Brandon stood chatting off to the side, drinks in hand as live music blared from down the street. Bruiser pulled Diem close and kissed her temple as they made their way toward the Ashe Crew who had come to show their support. Her chest filled with joy as she watched humans and shifters laughing and talking together.

The town she'd grown to love hadn't abandoned the bear shifters after all.

They'd just needed time to adjust to the idea that the supernatural did exist.

Her future with Boone stretched on and on. She was a wife now, a Keller, and a member of the Breck Crew. She had a family who would do anything to protect her. A family worth protecting. When her documentary had gone viral, and then was picked up by television stations, she'd turned down national news offers to stay at her job in this town where she could be with the ones she loved the most. And if the IESA ever came after her or any of the bear shifters again, there would be hell to pay from the humans determined to keep that agency accountable for their actions.

She was safe here under Boone's protection—under the shelter of the Breck Crew. Safe with the public who were making great strides to be accepting and protective of their fragile new alliance between humans and shifters.

And tonight, Boone would claim her. She and Rory would meet their bears for the first time, and it wasn't so scary anymore. She wasn't alone.

Cora swallowed a sob down as she looked up at her mate. "And here you thought bonding to me would be the end of both of our lives."

Boone kissed her lips, then rested his forehead against hers and brushed his knuckle across the tear stain on her cheek. "It turns out our bond was the beginning of something much better."

Want more of these characters?

Bear the Heat is the final book in a three book series called Fire Bears.

You can also read more about them in T. S. Joyce's Saw Bears series.

For more of these characters, check out these other books.

Bear My Soul
(Fire Bears, Book 1)

Bear the Burn
(Fire Bears, Book 2)

Up next in this universe...

Woodsman Werebear
Read on for a sneak peek

Chapter One

It came to Riley's attention two years too late she had terrible taste and worse luck in men.

Another knock pounded so hard against the doorframe, the vibration rattled a picture frame off the wall and shattered the glass across her tile floor. A pathetic whimper clawed its way up the back of her throat. With shaking hands, she threw another handful of clothes into the duffle bag on her bed

"Riley, let me the fuck in! That's my baby, too!"

"No, she's not! I've already explained that to you," Riley screamed. "She isn't yours, and she isn't mine."

"The baby is a she?" His voice dipped to a calmer, saner tone. "I don't care that you cheated when I was locked up, baby. I don't even care that you testified against me."

Bullshit. She wouldn't be fooled by Seamus Teague. Not this time. That man had the devil in him, and she was smarter now than when she'd been with him before.

"I have a restraining order, Seamus," she called out. "I'm calling the police." Again.

"No, you ain't. You already done called 'em twice tonight, and I'm betting they told you to give it a rest last time they paid you a visit. Let me in, baby. Come on." A soft, muffled sound filled the air, as if he was petting the door.

He was right, damn his cunning. She'd felt watched all night and could've sworn his best friend Jeremy's Toyota was parked in front of her apartment, but when the police had come out both times, Seamus was in the wind.

And now he was going to kill her.

The baby rolled inside the swell of her stomach. "Shhh," Riley cooed, rubbing her hand over her taut middle. "I won't let anything happen to you."

A fierce protectiveness washed over her as she straightened her spine and glared at the door. She wouldn't be one of his victims, and she sure as shit wasn't going to let this little angel be tainted by his poisonous love.

When she looked around her apartment, at the furniture she'd picked out and the dishes waiting in the clear glass cupboards her mom had gifted her when she'd moved in, a deep ache bloomed inside of her. She'd had a good life here until Seamus had messed everything up. The court, too, since they'd been the ones to make his sentence light enough that he was here, threatening her, rather than rotting away in prison as he deserved.

She wiped her sweating palms on her jeans and slid the strap of her duffle bag over her shoulder. Breath hitching and throat clogging with fear, she picked up a handgun she'd bought and learned how to use when she'd found out what a monster Seamus was.

All she had to do was make it out the main door where her friend April was waiting to drive her to the bus station. If she left now, she'd make one of the last buses leaving for the night, and Seamus would be delayed searching for her.

Checking the safety on her weapon, she padded to the door and threw it open wide.

Aiming the gun, she gritted out, "Get the fuck out

of my way, or I'll pull this trigger and dance on your fucking carcass."

Seamus's dark, empty eyes widened as if he was surprised—which was impossible because Seamus Teague didn't feel emotions, the cold-blooded snake. He lurched forward, grip barely missing her weapon, but she expected nothing less from him and jerked it out of his way, cocking the gun at the same time.

The crack of metal on metal stopped him, and slowly, he lifted his hands in surrender. A show, surely, because Seamus had never given up on anything as long as she'd known him. Riley gripped the handle harder to ease the tremble in her fingers, then twitched the gun impatiently. "I said move."

"Let's just discuss this like civilized people. That baby might not be blood related to me, but we're a family—"

"Move!" she screamed, the heat of fury blasting up her neck.

His snake-eyes narrowed, but he moved by inches, creating enough room in the doorway for her to get by.

Never turn your back on a predator. She backed down the hallway, weapon trained on the place where Seamus's heart should've been, if he had one.

His lip curled up in a snarl as he watched her leave. "It don't matter where you go, baby. And that restraining order don't mean shit to me. I'll find you no matter how long it takes to hunt you down. You got my baby in you now—my family."

"I told you," she murmured, swallowing a sob. "She ain't yours, and she ain't mine."

Her back hit the swinging exit door, so she turned and bolted for April's white Maxima parked right off the curb. Her friend had already thrown open the passenger's side door, bless her intuition.

Scream lodged in her throat, Riley slid into the car and shut the door as fast as she could before April peeled out of the parking lot.

When she looked behind her, Seamus was standing by the door, watching her leave with such hatred in his face, he looked like the monster he was inside. Twin tears rolled down her cheeks as she faced the front again. She had to stop doing that—looking back.

Looking back had stunted her ability to lead a better life when he'd been locked up.

Looking back had thrown her life into a

nightmare.

Looking back had kept her from healing from the horror she'd witnessed.

Riley nodded distractedly when April asked if she was all right.

She would be. Had to be.

Riley rubbed the tight swell of her belly and made another silent oath to protect the child she'd worked so hard to grow.

She'd talked on the phone to the biological parents of the baby she'd agreed to be a surrogate for, but this was the first time she would meet them in person.

And she sure as hell hoped Diem and Bruiser Keller were ready for the trouble that would be tailing her.

Woodsman Werebear

Available Now

About the Author

T.S. Joyce is devoted to bringing hot shifter romances to readers. Hungry alpha males are her calling card, and the wilder the men, the more she'll make them pour their hearts out. She werebear swears there'll be no swooning heroines in her books. It takes tough-as-nails women to handle her shifters.

Experienced at handling an alpha male of her own, she lives in a tiny town, outside of a tiny city, and devotes her life to writing big stories. Foodie, wolf whisperer, ninja, thief of tiny bottles of awesome smelling hotel shampoo, nap connoisseur, movie fanatic, and zombie slayer, and most of this bio is true.

Bear Shifters? Check

Smoldering Alpha Hotness? Double Check

Sexy Scenes? Fasten up your girdles, ladies and gents, it's gonna to be a wild ride.

For more information on T. S. Joyce's work,
visit her website at
www.tsjoyce.com